GUARD

A CROSS CREEK SMALL TOWN NOVEL

KELLY COLLINS

BOOK NOOK PRESS

Copyright © 2021 by Kelley Maestas

No part of this publication may be reproduced, distributed, or transmitted in any form or by any means, including photocopying, recording, or other electronic or mechanical methods, without the prior written permission of the publisher, except as permitted by U.S. copyright law. For permission requests, contact kelly@authorkellycollins.com.

The story, all names, characters, and incidents portrayed in this production are fictitious. No identification with actual persons (living or deceased), places, buildings, and products is intended or should be inferred. All products or brand names are trademarks of their respective owners.

CHAPTER ONE

ANGIE

CROSS CREEK MIGHT HOLD answers to my missing father's whereabouts.

I lifted my head as Roy said my name, like he'd called me several times. It took a second for me to break out of my thoughts and return to the counter of Roy's bar. He smiled, his kind eyes crinkling at the corners. "Where were you just then?" he asked.

I lifted both shoulders. "Sorry, I was a million miles away in my head." Nothing had gone according to plan. I thought I'd show up in Cross Creek, extract the town's secrets, figure out if my father was here, and if not, continue on my journey to find him. I didn't expect Ethan, and I certainly didn't plan on falling for him.

"Stop gawking at that Lockhart boy." Roy jerked his chin in the direction I'd been absentmindedly staring, and I followed the motion as my heartbeat raced like a horse in the Kentucky Derby. Ethan raised his beer in my direction with a smile before losing himself in his tablet. He was always focused on some kind of electronic device.

It all seemed like a good idea at first. I figured I could work for Roy on Kandra's days off to help lighten his load.

Where did people give up secrets? Bars.

Who could someone lean on when they were having a bad day? The bartender.

Me.

I ran my fingers through my hair to smooth it down as I watched Ethan's guarded expression. He stopped touching the screen and moved the tablet back as if to take in the entire image before him, and I wondered—for the millionth time—what kept him so captivated on the darn thing. I knew technology addiction was a real thing, but sheesh.

"Take him a beer, will ya?" Roy asked.

"Of course." I knew what the old man was up to, and it wouldn't work. I wasn't in Cross Creek for friendship or romance. I was here for *information*. And for Roy's famous garlic knots, that I ate without reserve.

Roy handed me a pint glass filled with chilled amber liquid. The scent of beer hit my nose, and I inhaled and wished for once that I could drink without concern. Scanning the room, I took in the place and its occupants. It was quiet for a Saturday.

Gypsy was there in her brightly colored butterfly shawl, blue leggings that replaced her flowing summer skirts, and her tie-dyed river-colored blouse. She was a throwback from the day when people drove VW Vans graffitied with peace signs and flowers—when a daisy chain was something you put in your hair and not a sexual act. Over the last several months, she and Roy had become inseparable, and it was heartwarming to watch love bloom. The idea filled me with happiness and a tad dose of jealousy.

Patti sat near Gypsy and waved at me. She didn't come in

often, but when she did, she and Gypsy usually talked and laughed for hours. They were fun to listen to and watch. Kind of like a scene from Thelma and Louise, but never taking the friendship over the cliff.

Ethel and Norman were in their booth, and every time Ethel would say something, Norman would reply with a loud "Huh?" They shared a batch of garlic knots and laughter that brought a smile to my lips as I made my way to Ethan with his beer.

Benji sat in a corner; his shoulders curled inward as if he was in time out. The town had kind of put him there after his destructive behavior toward Kandra. While Kandra had become the town sweetheart, Benji was busy trying to right his wrongs and fix his reputation. A person didn't write lies about someone in the paper and get away with it. He'd been doing well, volunteering his time to help others and all around being a better person. Tonight, though, he wasn't alone. Some young man sat with him—a good-looking guy with blond hair, bright eyes, and an uncanny resemblance to Benji. A brother, maybe?

The stranger's gaze met mine, and he nodded. I offered a friendly smile and turned my attention to Ethan as I set his beer before him. Something in Ethan's deep blue eyes seemed troubled, and I took a seat across from him, glancing over my shoulder at Roy. Since business was slow, I doubted he'd mind if I took a moment. Besides, Roy was a laid-back boss and encouraged conversation. He always had that "put people first" attitude, and it made me wonder what kind of father he'd be.

"You seem unhappy." I reached out and hooked a finger over the top of his tablet. Pushing the device toward the table, I noticed his eyes narrow as they met mine. "Whatcha up to?"

"Working." His sour tone didn't faze me. I knew how grumpy

he could be, but I didn't mind. There was something about Ethan that always drew me in. It was like we had a soul connection, but I doubt he recognized that because his focus was always elsewhere.

"So, what are you working on?" I tried to lower the tablet more to look at the screen, but he pulled it toward himself and pushed a button. The screen went black, and I pressed my lips together. "I want to see."

His facial features relaxed. "Really?"

I nodded and leaned in like I was sharing a secret. "I'll try not to steal your super-secret designs." I caught glimpses here and there, and it always seemed like architectural plans of some sort.

He chuckled and turned the screen back on. It flared to life, and he flipped the device around.

I studied the lines and measurements. Glossing over the numbers and equations, I took in the entire image. The building was beautiful.

"Is this your dream mansion on the edge of a cliff once you become rich and famous?" I smiled at him, knowing he wasn't that type of guy at all. He didn't have a flashy or show-off bone in his body, and I liked that about him. Instead, he had that down-to-earth charm that warmed my insides like hot cocoa on a snowy winter day.

He shook his head and glanced over his drawing. "No, this one's for fun."

"You could give Frank Lloyd Wright a run for his money." I studied the image again, loving the high roofs, the glass features, and the beautiful angles. It might only be a sketch, but I could imagine the absolute modern palace the finished building would be. Tucked into the edge of the forest would be magnificent.

He lit up. "What makes you say that?"

I inhaled, trying to put my thoughts into words. "Well, Frank Lloyd Wright was a visionary, an incredible architect, and he changed the way we live and build. And this," I touched the edge of his tablet, "is world's better than anything of his I've ever seen."

Ethan's eyes danced with delight, and a smile tugged his lips. All the shadows in his expression faded, and his eyes crinkled at the corners. "Thank you," he whispered.

"You're very welcome, but I meant every word. So, how have you been?" I wanted to know more and having his undivided attention was intoxicating.

"Good, good. My brothers are all busy now that they've found love." He chuckled, but I sensed some shred of honest bitterness. Maybe he was upset he hadn't found anyone yet.

Talk of his family twisted my gut. I wished I had a family I could talk about, but my mother and I weren't on speaking terms.

My eyes stung, and I blinked rapidly to send the tears back that threatened to spill. I wouldn't think about my mother or the dysfunction she brought to my life. "You'll meet someone … if you haven't already." I couldn't think about that, either. I liked Ethan—a lot. Still, I wasn't here to find love, and I needed to keep my head on straight. The answers were close, and I couldn't give up my quest until I knew the truth.

As much as it hurt to think about, dividing my attention between the reason I came to Cross Creek and trying to win Ethan's affections was slowing down my search. I needed to remember why I was here, which meant cooling my jets with Ethan, the Lockhart boy with the troubled eyes and killer smile. At least, I'd do my best to redirect my attention.

With that, I stood up and headed toward the counter once more—no need to take advantage of Roy's kindness. The second I locked eyes with him, I knew I needn't have worried; his enormous smile told me it thrilled him that I was talking to Ethan.

I smiled back at him. I spent a lot of time building relationships with everyone in town and had been doing everything possible to dig into people's pasts without drawing too much suspicion. Somehow, I still had no definitive answers. Well, I had one. I wasn't a Lockhart. Though stealing hairs from all the brothers and having them tested made me feel creepy, it proved I wasn't the love child of Kip and my mother.

All the information I gleaned seemed to point to Roy as the most likely candidate to be my father. As I hesitated, Roy gestured with a wave of his hand for me to go back to Ethan's table.

Why not? I turned back, and the young man from Benji's table appeared at my elbow. "Hey," he said in a low voice.

"Hey back," I answered, as friendly as always. My mind wasn't on this stranger; it was on the heavy topic that had been at the forefront of my thoughts for months. I needed to figure out who my father was. I needed to know who I was and where I came from and why my body was failing me. Just having someone to share the challenges with would be amazing. Hopefully that someone would want me in their life.

"Can we get a couple more beers?" He glanced back at Benji, who was still hunched forward, head down, looking beaten by the world.

"Sure." I turned back to Roy as the guy grabbed my arm right above the elbow. Offering a friendly and confused smile, I turned to face him once more. "Did you need something else?"

"What's a girl like you doing working in a dump like this?" His serious expression told me this was an honest attempt to hit on me using the weakest pickup line I'd heard in a long time.

"Well, I like this place, and I wouldn't call it a dump," I said with a soft laugh. Part of me felt terrible for the guy. Flirting wasn't his strongest suit, and since I wasn't the type of girl to bring anyone down, I was nice instead. "But thanks." I understood his sentiment, even if I disagreed. To someone that didn't know the town, this place might look like a total dive. I wouldn't excuse his rudeness, but I could understand his error.

"Well, if you're ever in Silver Springs, hit me up." He offered me his number on a napkin, and I took it with no intention of calling.

"I didn't know people still wrote numbers down," I blurted out, then covered my awkward omission by taking out my phone. "I'll put your number in now. What's your name?"

"Clark."

I pretended to key in his name and number, then thanked him. "It's great meeting you, Clark." I gestured with my phone to show I was thanking him for his number, then headed back to the bar to grab him and Benji a drink. Hurrying to drop them off at the table, I made polite small talk, but my mind was back to pondering how my mother had lied to me about everything.

She told me that my father died in the war, that he was Native American, and I was tribe royalty. There were so many lies stacked on mistruths and covered with misdeeds. I didn't hate my mom, but she made my life more difficult with her dishonesty. I only discovered the truth when I took a DNA test to trace my heritage and found out I was not Native American at all, but a hodgepodge of European with a little Greek thrown in for flavor. As usual, she stuck to her lies when I questioned her. She told me the test was wrong, and they swapped the results all the time, or the people who sent the results had lied. Her doubt in the system made me pluck not only Ethan's hair but all his brothers' too. One result might be faulty, but four wouldn't lie.

It didn't serve me well to argue because once Mom got an idea into her head, it was trapped until she let it go. That wasn't the worst of my mother's lies … but it was all I was prepared to deal with right now.

"Call me," Clark said as I left the table. I nodded, knowing full well I had no intention of calling him, and headed back toward Ethan's table where he was back on his tablet.

"You know, you work an awful lot. Would it kill you to take some time off?" I smiled at him.

He seemed oddly upset as his gaze met mine. It was the same look my first-grade teacher gave me when I ate the red Play-Doh—a look of total disappointment.

"Uh-oh, I know that look. What's on your mind?" I sat down beside him, but he shifted, moving his body away from me in a gesture that stung. It took me back to third grade when Helen Huntsmen wouldn't sit next to me at lunch because she said I smelled like old lady's perfume. She was right, because Grams had smothered me with hugs that morning, but it still hurt.

"First my brother, now someone else?" He tipped his chin toward Clark, who seemed to watch us.

"What?" I didn't understand what he was getting at. My head filled with fog, as if the stress of the last few months caught up with me.

He took a gulp of his beer, then set the empty glass down with a thud. "I'm tired of being chosen last."

What he said clicked. It upset him that Clark gave me his number. How could I tell him I was just being nice? That I had no intention of ever calling the guy and had summarily tossed his number away. I wasn't interested in the person who used the worst pickup line in history. Then again, why did I have to explain myself? It wasn't as if Ethan had ever asked me out. We weren't dating, and I was free to see whoever I damn well pleased.

The emotions of the last several months overflowed, and I lashed out. "I've always chosen you first, Ethan. Maybe your head's been too buried in your tablet to notice."

"Maybe, but I've always wondered why you came to Cross Creek." His serious gaze and the gravity of the comment stopped me short. "What do we have to offer you here?"

I wouldn't be my mother and lie, but I needed to be careful how I answered. "I came here looking for something." No way I'd tell him the whole truth. Not yet. I rose and walked away.

CHAPTER TWO

ETHAN

I COULD STILL SEE the longing in her eyes when she told me she was in Cross Creek looking for something. Why didn't she admit she was looking for love? Maybe she didn't want to confess that out loud. Still, I hadn't liked seeing her flirt with that guy. I was tired of being chosen last for everything. My brothers were all finding love, and yet, I was alone.

She told me she always chose me first, but I was too buried in my tablet to notice. Was she right? Was I so deeply invested in work that I didn't see what happened around me?

"What are you thinking about right now?" Max asked as he sat at the kitchen table beside me. I invited him over for some coffee, but that was a farce. The beloved mailman delivered more than mail, and I needed his guidance.

Losing my father left a hole in my heart. I still couldn't believe Dad hadn't told anyone about his heart troubles until the very end. There was no chance for me to come to terms with his passing before the fact. Instead, I'd been left to pick up the pieces. The worst feeling was being unable to forgive someone for not telling you something. No, that's not true. The worst feeling was being unable to forgive someone for not telling you the whole truth and not being able to talk to them about how that had hurt you. There was no closure.

My dad was a great man. He taught me it was okay for men to have feelings and express them, and there was no shame in getting help. Why hadn't he taken his own advice and let me or my brothers in? He left us in the dark.

I stared into my coffee. "Why didn't Dad tell me he was sick?"

Max sighed. "I'm sure he had his reasons. Health is a difficult topic, and I doubt he wanted to hurt you or make you worry. Maybe he wanted the last time he had with you and your family to be special and not overshadowed with concern and fear for his well-being. When people know you're sick, they don't treat you the same."

I'd like to believe that I would've treated him the same, but he didn't give me the chance. "Am I an awful person for not being able to forgive him for that?" I glanced at Max and noticed the sheen of moisture in his eyes as he stared at something I instinctively knew wasn't in the room with us.

"Forgiveness is a fickle mistress. I can tell you from personal experience you can't force forgiveness and shouldn't beat yourself up about it." Max's voice seemed thin, and I wanted to hug him. Instead, I settled for giving him an awkward shoulder pat.

It occurred to me I knew little about Max's history before Cross Creek. As if reading my mind, he spoke. "Did you know I left Cross Creek for a while?"

I wanted to hear his story. "Why?" Max always had a way of

helping me with my issues through his tales. If this was a chance to return the favor, I was all in.

He shook his head as if he wasn't willing to share that part of himself. "I needed to get away and clear my head. I can promise you that forgiveness is an issue you have to work through alone. No one can do it for you. Those around you can help show you the way, but they can't take the journey." He reached out and squeezed my shoulder, then pulled me in for a tight hug that had me blinking back tears. After a firm pat on my back, he let go.

"Does it get easier?" I asked. "You know … to forgive?"

He shook his head. "I don't know."

My heart sank. Whatever he was holding on to, he obviously hadn't forgiven himself for yet.

Given the heaviness in the room, a subject change was in order.

"I think I really like Angie." I shook my head. Like wasn't a strong enough word, but love was too bold. How could I love her when she seemed to love everyone else in town? "But she's such a big flirt, and I don't know if I can handle it."

Max chuckled. "Relationships are difficult, son. If you try to force her to be someone—or something—she's not, then you have to ask yourself if you truly love her. That doesn't mean she's not allowed to have traits that drive you crazy. The question is, can you live with them? Have you ever asked yourself why she flirts? Unmet needs drive most of our actions."

I leaned back in my chair and thought about his words. "She flirted with my brother, and she did it to make me notice her."

He inhaled. "Well, maybe she doesn't have the tools to do things differently. Or maybe you're not the easiest person to reach." He gave me a significant stare, and I wondered if anyone had ever called me out so harshly.

With a gulp of my coffee, I watched him lift the plain white mug to his lips while he glanced around the room.

I stared at the home I'd built from the ground up, and while it had everything a house could have, from the best appliances to high-end furnishings, it felt cold. It was missing something—the warmth of a companion.

Contemplating his words, I wondered if he was right. Was it that she didn't know how else to get through to me? What were her unmet needs? Was I part of that equation? As flattering as it was that she'd gone out of her way to make me jealous, it also bothered me. It was as if she knew me well and not at all.

"I dated a flirty woman once, and it was too much for me. I'm not the jealous type, and I could've lived with her flirting, but there were other traits I couldn't handle." His attention returned to his mug, and he stared into it for a moment as if it held all the answers we both needed. "Even though she and I didn't work out, I still found my wife. The right woman is waiting for you."

My head jerked up, and I stared at Max. *His wife?* He never mentioned it in all the time I'd known him. "I had no idea you were married."

Max nodded. "Yep, before I came to Cross Creek. Coming here was my attempt at starting over. What I'm trying to tell you is that you can heal from anything. If someone has traits you can't live with, don't force it, but remember, we all have flaws." He glanced at the tablet on my table. "Decide where your priorities sit."

Max was trying to divert attention back to my situation, but it still stunned me to learn he'd been married. He said he came to

Cross Creek to start over. Had they divorced? Maybe it was an ugly, painful split, and he didn't want to think about it. Whatever happened, it'd been enough to keep him from remarrying.

I realized how little I knew about the man who'd been like a father to me since my father passed, and guilt tugged at my insides. What if Max needed as much support and advice as he gave? Maybe he was the one with unmet needs—a man who wanted an understanding ear. In this town, who listened to Max?

"You know, I'm here if you ever need or want to talk." I stood up and stretched to hide the painful lump in my throat and the ache consuming my gut.

"I appreciate that offer." His thick voice made me avoid his gaze because I didn't want to see the pain in his tone mirrored in his eyes. "What's your next step with Angie?" he asked.

"I'm not sure." Could I handle her flirtatious personality? I didn't doubt she had feelings for me. She'd gone to great lengths to get my attention. Unless attention was her endgame. If we were going to be together, I wanted to be the only man in her life. "She seemed so surprised when I told her I was tired of being chosen last."

"Maybe that's what you need to do; be open and honest about your feelings and expectations." Max sounded more like his usual self, but I didn't dare look at him. Instead, I fixed my attention on a spot on the wall. I wasn't sure if it was a spider or some speck of dirt. I'd investigate when Max left. If it was dirt, I'd clean it. If it was a spider, I'd put it outside.

"When you said that to her, what did she say?" Max asked.

The speck was absolutely a spider because I was sure I'd seen it move. "She told me she's always chosen me first, but I've been too buried in my tablet to notice."

"Ouch. Maybe she's on to something. You are busy more often than not. What I said goes both ways. She can't want to change you and say she loves you either. Either she can live with you the way you are, or she can't." Max lifted a shoulder and let it drop right away. "As for being chosen last ... don't forget you always save the best for last."

"Last for everything from sports teams to my place in the family business."

"Maybe that's because you're the brains and your brothers are the brawn."

"Not true, Quinn is the numbers guy and probably the smartest of us all."

"But you're the creative one which means you think with a different side of your brain. The side that's also more sensitive. Stop placing yourself in a position that no one else has. Maybe that's your flaw. She said she put you first. Believe her."

"Is there a way we can grow together?" I didn't like the thought that we had flaws that pitted us against one another.

"That's the idea. I didn't mean you had to accept each other's shortcomings. I'm trying to say that you can't force the other to change or go into a relationship intending to change the other. She has to want that, and so do you." Max's tone had that far away quality again, and I wondered if he was thinking about his ex-wife.

"I should get going." He stood up and offered his hand. "It's been a pleasure."

I shook it, then pulled him in for a hug.

"Thank you," I said before letting him go. "These talks mean a lot to me." More than I could ever vocalize, primarily because of that pesky, aching lump in my throat. I wished my dad was here to mentor me, but Max was excellent at giving the advice I needed.

"Don't beat yourself up." Max smiled at me as we headed for the front door. "Life is hard, so try not to add to the difficulty." As I pulled the door open, the chill slipped right past my sweater and bit into my skin.

Max shivered and gave a warm smile. "The cold season is upon us."

"I guess so. Have a good day, Max." I waved goodbye as he left and closed the door behind him. Pulling my phone out of my pocket, I texted Noah first.

Did you know Max was married? I wandered to my couch and sat down as I waited for his response. I didn't have to wait long.

No. He never told me that.

Maybe Bayden would know something. I propped my feet up on the coffee table and got comfortable before texting him. *Do you know anything about Max's marriage?*

Max was married?

Apparently, Bayden didn't know either. No way Quinn would know anything. Everybody knew not to trust him with a secret. He was like the town crier. If you wanted everyone to know something, you told Quinn.

I don't want to speculate because that feels disrespectful, but I'll ask him. Noah's text made me nod. I didn't want to jump to conclusions either.

I'll talk to him next time I see him. Clearly, Bayden had the same thought.

Has anyone messaged Quinn? I hit send and stared at the black TV screen across the room. I wasn't sure why I bought the thing, because I never used it. It was more or less a dust magnet.

No, Bayden replied.

Nope. Noah texted.

He's not the best at keeping secrets, I typed back. And just like that, we silently agreed to keep this from our brother. Not because we didn't love him, but because he didn't need to know, and we didn't want the entire town to be privy to Max's secret.

I loved my brother, but loose lips sink ships. Putting my phone away, I pulled out my tablet and sketched an idea that had been tickling at the edges of my mind since I'd woken up out of a dream I couldn't remember but knowing somewhere deep inside that it left me feeling safe and loved.

As the lines took shape, I lost myself in the angles and math.

In my head, I could see Angie's brown eyes as she spoke to me at Roy's. "Well, *Frank Lloyd Wright was a visionary, an incredible architect, and he changed the way we live and build. And this is world's better than anything of his I've ever seen.*"

CHAPTER THREE

ANGIE

I STRETCHED to hang the string of Christmas lights over the hook. Just a little farther, I told myself. Roy had told me to stay off the ladder while he delivered an order of pizza, but it wasn't in my nature to sit on my butt when there was work to be done.

With a groan, I reached a little more, stretching until the string of lights on my fingertips finally slid onto the hook, and I let out a sigh of relief. Relaxing my body slightly, I felt the ladder shift under me and grabbed it with both hands.

A nervous laugh escaped my lips, and I tried to calm my galloping heart. The universe tilted as the ladder skimmed along the wall. Unable to keep my balance, I let out a sharp scream as the ground rushed at me.

Squeezing my eyes closed, I waited for pain as the ladder crashed to the ground, but I didn't. Arms caught me and cradled me tightly to a powerful chest. I opened one eye, peeking up at Ethan, and couldn't hold back a smile.

"Hi." I sounded breathless, but I wasn't afraid. I'd felt worse hurt in my life than a ladder could dish out.

He didn't seem to appreciate my calm.

"What the hell were you doing up there?"

I glanced at the wall, the string of lights, the ladder now on the ground, and looked back at him. "Do I need to answer that?"

He set me on my feet and picked up the ladder. Placing it against the wall before glaring at me. "I don't want you up on this thing again."

I shoved my hands into the back pockets of my jeans and lifted both shoulders. "Okay, then you tell Roy I can't do my job." It was a bluff; hanging lights wasn't part of my job. It was busy work to keep me from being bored on a slow Sunday evening. The bar was empty except for Ethan and me. I guess everyone had better plans than coming here.

He let out a growl of displeasure and climbed up the ladder. "Are you hanging them over the hooks?"

"Yep." I picked up the window dressings. Those were easier because all I had to do was attach the silver garland to the hooks in the top of the windows, and the multicolored decorative bulbs would hang at varying lengths next to the glass. No ladder required. "Thanks for your help and thank you for not bringing up the ladder incident when Roy gets back."

"Where is he?" He looked down at me, leaving me unsure if he was going to tell Roy after all.

"He's delivering a pizza." I fiddled with a glittery silver bulb, mesmerized as it reflected the Christmas lights Ethan was hanging.

"You were up on the ladder while you were here alone?" His incredulous tone had me widening my eyes.

Why did everyone think I shouldn't be doing things alone? Maybe they weren't wrong in this one instance, but I'd never fallen off a ladder before in my life. And this time, I would've been fine if Ethan hadn't been creeping in and out of my thoughts all afternoon. He was knocking me off my game. "If a job needs to be done, I'm going to do it."

"What if you'd fallen and gotten hurt?" He sounded angry, but I sensed he was upset about the situation, not at me.

"Look, I'm fine. I don't need you to come barging in here like some Prince Charming and sweep me off my feet, or whatever that was." Not going to lie, it was a tempting thought.

He snorted in disbelief. "Oh yeah? Obviously, you had everything under control." With careful steps, he made his way down the ladder. His shirt rode up, showing off his powerful body, and I had to stare. Any girl with working ovaries couldn't look away.

"How do you know falling wasn't part of my plan? I saved a few moments and made it to the ground faster than you did." I nodded at him as he stepped off the ladder to the floor and made his way to me. I set the garland down and straightened up as we came face-to-face.

"This isn't a joke, Angie." He pointed at the ladder. "Safety first, always."

I lifted two fingers to my forehead and gave a brief salute. "Yes, sir." Glancing past him, I noticed he'd finished stringing the lights. "Thank you," I said.

"For saving you from broken bones?" His intense stare made something flutter low in my belly.

I shook my head. "For finishing hanging the lights. I did most of the work, though." With that, I stepped back and snatched up the garland as he chuckled.

"You're unbelievable." He shoved his fingers through his dark hair, parting it in new places. Somehow, he still looked good, as always.

"Thanks." I stood up on the seat of the booth and hung one side of the garland. Without prompting, he moved to the other side and hung it.

"It wasn't a compliment." His stare still had that intensity that was messing with my ability to breathe.

I shrugged. "It sounded like a compliment." My heart rate was finally winding down, and my hands seemed to stop shaking. The near miss had rattled me, and as much as I was teasing Ethan, I was glad he came to my rescue.

Side by side, we hung up more lights. "I used to want to be the Grinch," I said.

He glanced at me curiously.

Staring up at the garland as we hung it, I grinned. "The thought of living alone with my dog and only seeing people once a year ... that sounded like the life."

"Antisocial kid, huh?" He asked, fixing his side and untangling the strings of two bulbs. When they hung freely, we moved to the next window.

I glanced at him. "Kid? Sure." I didn't ever remember doing anything other kids did. I had to grow up fast and pretty much on my own. My mom made it hard to have friends. She didn't like other kids hanging around. Maybe it was because no one else swallowed her lies like me. She didn't want people around that called her on her bullshit. Still, that was too sad a story to share with Ethan. It wasn't like I had it that bad. I mean, some people's parents beat them. My mother never laid a hand on me. She just lied—a lot—about everything.

"I love the holidays. Lights, holiday treats, the decorations..." Ethan trailed off, and I glanced at him, surprised.

"You like shiny things?" Ethan liked the holidays? The Ethan I knew seemed guarded and serious all the time with his head buried in work. He didn't come across as someone full of holiday cheer.

He glanced at me as if he shared something he didn't mean to and lowered his head. "Yeah." His sheepish tone made his confession cuter.

I took a step closer to him and gazed up into his eyes. "I love that," I said, taking his hands in mine. My heart took off with the swiftness of an owl's wings in winter. The quiet of the moment sank into my soul as I stared at him. We were so close I could rise on my tiptoes and press my lips to his if I wanted, and I did want to.

My lips tingled as if expecting contact. His gaze lowered to my mouth, then met mine, and I exhaled and reached for him.

"Did you hang the lights, anyway?" Roy's tone slashed through the mood, and I jumped away from Ethan. Running a hand over the back of my neck, I tried to calm down. I almost kissed Ethan. At work, in front of the windows, in full view of anyone driving by, I almost kissed him.

"Ethan helped." I couldn't look at him, so I stared at the floor instead. What an awkward moment for Roy to show back up. Had he seen us through the windows? I doubted it; no way he would've interrupted us if he knew we were about to kiss. Roy was like old man cupid with the way he kept pushing me toward this particular Lockhart brother.

Ethan cleared his throat.

"I guess I'll have to add him to the payroll." Roy's cheerful tone echoed through the silent bar.

"My contribution wouldn't even cover my tab," Ethan said.

I giggled; well aware the bar didn't have tabs.

"What tab?" Roy's quick grin and humor were infectious as he glanced from me to Ethan.

"Exactly." Ethan settled into a seat and folded his hands in front of him.

I could feel his stare, but there was no way I could meet it. I almost kissed him.

Before Ethan could explain why he had to step in and help me, I spoke up. "Don't forget I'm not coming in tomorrow."

Roy nodded as if he remembered. "I know. You're fine, and I hope you have a good time." I hadn't told him why I wasn't working, but I absolutely wouldn't be having a good time.

Ethan chimed in. "Why aren't you coming to work?"

My heart sank, and I leaned against the bar. Looking at my folded arms, I blurted out more information than I meant to. "I'm going to Silver Springs." Everything in my body told me not to say anything, but I had to give him some explanation. A question could not go unanswered, but I already said too much.

"Oh yeah? I've been putting off a trip to Silver Springs. They have this shop that sells..." He stopped talking and let out a chuckle before continuing, "never mind, boring work stuff. I'd be happy to go with you."

Ethan's hopeful tone filled me with white-hot terror.

"Oh, no. That won't work." The words burst out of me.

Roy let out a grumble, and I glanced over at him. "I'll be right back. Keep an eye on the front for me, okay?" He nodded at the door before leaving.

"Why not?" Ethan sounded confused. "You don't want me to

come with you?"

With every brain cell screaming *fire* and running in circles, I desperately struggled for some excuse for why he couldn't come with me. This was bad. I said far too much, now I was acting suspiciously. Ethan had to know something was up.

I flashed a smile I didn't feel and ran my fingers through my hair. "It's not that. I'm going to a hair appointment which will take *hours*." I hated lying to him, but what other option did I have? I couldn't tell him the truth. Not because I didn't trust him—I absolutely did—but because I couldn't bear for him to know. This was one secret I had to keep no matter what. Everything was tied together. My illness. My father. It was like a tangled string of lights that I couldn't unravel.

"Oh." Somehow he made one word sound like *I don't believe you, maybe you're telling the truth*, and *I'm disappointed* all at once.

"Maybe another time?" I said, disappointed that the entire mood of the evening seemed ruined. We'd been having fun, and now everything was back to being strained between us. I hated the change.

"Sure." He didn't sound sure at all. No, he sounded like he was shutting down—there was no color to his voice, nothing warm in his features, and his eyes narrowed. He was upset, and it was my fault. Why did I open my stupid mouth?

I had come a breath away from kissing him only a few minutes before, and now it was as if a chasm materialized between us. My heart ached, and I wanted to take it all back. I wished I could rewind to the almost-kiss and do the rest over. I would have stretched until our lips met.

At least he hadn't told Roy I'd fallen off the ladder.

CHAPTER FOUR

ETHAN

WHAT WAS she doing in Silver Springs, and why was she against me going with her?

I didn't mind waiting for her hair appointment, but she hadn't given me the option. Spending time with her was my real motivation for going, and she put the kibosh on that mighty quickly.

Was she meeting the guy who gave her his number? I heard him tell her if she was ever in Silver Springs she should hit him up.

I stared at the project I was supposed to be working on, but nothing was coming to me. Work had never been difficult; this was a new problem, and I didn't like it. Given it was Monday, and I had things to do, not working was wearing on me. I flung my tablet to the side, and it bounced on the couch beside me as I stared at the TV screen.

The feeling of her in my arms killed me in the best possible way. I caught her like some damn hero in a sappy movie when she fell off the ladder, yet my relationship with Angie was anything but that kind of sticky, sweet, uncomplicated romance.

She almost kissed me. Hell, when Roy walked in I was profoundly disappointed. I wanted her to kiss me. Stretching my legs out, I rested my feet on the coffee table and glared at my tablet. My brain was anywhere but work. The sweet smell of her and the warmth radiating off her skin was more intoxicating than any drink I ever tasted. Her soft smile and the pure electric excitement sparkling in her eyes when she stared up at me were like a song on repeat in my head.

Was that another attempt to flirt? She seemed to have backed off from flirting with me. Maybe she teased to boost her self-esteem. Perhaps knowing people wanted her made her happy. I didn't enjoy thinking she used me to stroke her ego.

I picked up my tablet and turned on the screen. The graceful lines of my design lied, and the math didn't seem to work out. With careful thought and attention, I tried again, but I slipped right back to her shining eyes as she lifted on tiptoes and licked her lips. That same thrilling jolt tightened my stomach. I was an idiot for letting jealousy eat away at me. My gut burned like I'd ingested battery acid.

Angie wasn't like that. I'd known her for a while, and all signs pointed to her being a good person. I was projecting my fears of being overlooked when it was likely something innocent on her part. She was getting her hair done and didn't want me bored and waiting for her. After all, she didn't seem into that Clark guy. She virtually ignored him, instead sitting with me and commenting on my work.

Would she have kissed me if she planned to see someone else the next day? No way.

I had no proof she was doing anything awful, but why did my gut tell me she'd been lying when she said she was getting her hair done? I always had that sixth sense about things. I called it intuition. My brothers called it paranoia.

I erased the work I'd been trying to fix. The numbers weren't adding up, and I made a mess of a partial idea that wasn't coming together. Not being able to work would drive me crazy. I considered a walk to clear my head, but the chill outside made me want to stay indoors and crank up the heat another notch.

Maybe I'd been reading her wrong. The near-miss kiss might have meant nothing to her, but it was a big deal to me.

Feeling the chill in the air, I made my way to the thermostat and turned up the heat before walking to the door. The frosted glass revealed why it was freezing in my house; the first snow of the year was piling up outside.

The fluffy white banks were already nearly a foot deep. I stood there, staring into the enormous white drifting flakes, thinking about my father. He taught me to shovel our steps and our neighbors. My brothers and I had taken that advice to heart, and we'd each pick a side of the road and a direction and clear the entire neighborhood.

Dad's vision was that if one person slipped, fell, and wound up hurt, then that person wouldn't be available for their place in our community; be it working at the doctor's office, the salon, the grocery store, or the kind old lady that knitted hats for everyone in town. No matter who we were helping, that person had some place in our community. We'd notice them missing if they could no longer take part in our day-to-day lives. By helping each other out, the community stayed strong.

That paralyzing ache of loss froze my lungs, and no matter

how hard I tried, I couldn't draw a breath. I thought about the snow shovel in my garage and went to put on my thermals to carry on the legacy my father had taught me.

As I walked toward my bedroom, my phone rang. I answered it to hear Angie's breathless voice.

"Hey, sorry to bother you," she said.

I stopped in place, worry filling my veins.

"Are you okay?" Her tone made me believe she wasn't.

She let out a shaky laugh. "Yeah, but my car slid into a snowbank." The incredulous tone of her voice told me she couldn't believe this had happened. "I was just so tired from my appointment..." She trailed off, and I wondered how a hair appointment could be exhausting. "Anyway, I'm stuck and need help."

My heart sank, and I rushed toward the front door and grabbed my coat. "Where are you?"

"I'm on Oak Road, about a block from home." The wobble in her words warned me she was on the verge of tears. "I was so close."

"I'll be there shortly." Grabbing my keys, I headed out the door, locked it behind me, and crunched my way through the snow-pack to my truck.

"Ethan?" She said my name quietly, and every hair on my arms stood up. "Are you still there?"

"Yes?" Pulling open my door, I climbed inside the cab and turned over the engine while considering what I'd need to tow her car. Everything, including the cables and winch, was in the back.

"Please don't hang up," she said.

"I won't." Turning on my phone's Bluetooth, I connected the device to talk hands-free. "I'll drive slowly, so I make it to you safely. The roads are terrible." I couldn't believe how many inches had already fallen. "Are you warm enough?"

"Yeah, I'm in the car with the heater on. It's not bad; I'm just stuck." Her laugh didn't calm my pounding heart. "Thank you for doing this."

"It's not a problem." I made my way through the heavy snowfall. The silent streets were empty and eerie, and her voice echoed in my cab, guiding me to her like a moth to a flame.

"I should've put my chains on, but I was so close to home that I thought I had it."

"It's easy to slide on the ice and snow." It was a simple mistake. Personally, I was glad she was okay. "I'm happy you're not hurt."

Momentary silence stretched between us before her soft words flowed from my truck speakers. "I like knowing you care."

As she spoke, my headlights lit up the back end of her car. "Stay put. I see you." I drove past her, parked in front, and got out of my truck, heading through the thick snow toward her.

I bent down and dug out the front of her little car. She was right. It wasn't that bad. There wasn't any damage to her bumper.

I held up one finger, telling her to give me a moment, and walked over the packed snow my tires had left. At the back of my truck, I grabbed my tow strap and hooked it to my hitch.

Walking the line toward her car, I knelt in the freezing snow and secured it around the frame. With a swift tug, I made sure it was tight before making my way to her passenger door. I tugged it open, and a whoosh of hot air mixed with her floral scent wafted past me.

"You're all hooked up. I didn't see any damage to the bumper. I'm just going to keep you hooked up and make sure you get home."

She nodded, her lips curving into a slight smile at the news.

"Has someone ever towed you before?" I didn't like the thought of her first time being in these conditions, but I didn't know what choice we had. With the snow continuing to build, we had to get her home.

"Yep." She nodded. "I'm the brakes."

I breathed a sigh of relief. "Yes. Okay, we'll move slowly."

Her wide eyes locked on mine, and all I saw was trust. "Okay." At that moment, I would've sworn she'd follow me anywhere, and that made me feel superhuman.

I shook myself free of that thought and opened the door. "See you on the other side," I said, closing it behind me. She smiled and flashed a thumbs-up. With a chuckle, I walked through the biting cold back to my truck. The heater hit me like a blowtorch, and my icy hands felt like they were being pierced with nails.

I looked both ways on the empty street and slowly pulled forward. My truck didn't seem to notice her car. It was as if the weight didn't matter. I pulled her out of the drift and onto the road. "Yay," she said, and I startled, forgetting we hadn't hung up our phone call.

"You all right back there?" I glanced in my rearview mirror, seeing her clutch her steering wheel like it was a lifeline.

"All right? I'm freaking thrilled. I'm not stuck, and I'm on my way home. I owe you one." The relief in her voice brought a smile to my lips. I wondered if this would count towards Dad's good deeds lesson.

"You don't owe me anything." Dad would've told me this was the right thing to do, and I agreed. What had coming out here cost me? A few minutes of time and a couple of dollars in gas? Maybe, but who gave a damn about a couple of bucks and a little time?

"You're a good man, Ethan Lockhart."

Her words warmed me, and I focused on the road and the ever-deepening snow. "Don't tell anyone," I joked.

She lowered her voice like we were swapping secrets. "Hate to break the news, but they already know."

"Damn." As we pulled up to her home, my heart squeezed. I wasn't ready to say good night or for our time together to be over. "We're here." With that, I parked my truck, slid out of the driver's seat into the snow, and went to unhook the two straps. She was at her car, taking off the strap there.

We met in the middle, and she smiled up at me with those incredible shining eyes. "I'm so grateful for your help."

I was still worried about her. "Are you sure you're okay?" An accident without damage or injury could still be mentally devastating.

She pressed her lips together, and when she released them, they became cherry red. "I'm okay, thanks to you."

"I was simply doing the right thing."

"It means a lot." We stood toe-to-toe with her eyes locked on mine. The way her face tilted in the low light and how the snowflakes floated around her left me breathless. She was impossibly beautiful—almost ethereal.

She rose on her tiptoes and threw her arms around me. "You're the best," she whispered in my ear.

"I was more than happy to help." I wound my arms around her and hugged her tightly. Instead of releasing me, she clung for a few moments. The scent of shampoo and her shiny hair brought a smile to my lips. "Your hair looks beautiful."

"Thank you," she whispered right before her lips met mine. Warmth surged through my body. Before I could fully process that she was kissing me, she lowered and spun around, hurrying for her front door.

Holy hell. She kissed me. Angie kissed me, and my lips still tingled from the touch.

CHAPTER FIVE

ANGIE

AFTER GETTING stuck and kissing Ethan, I'd hidden for a full twenty-four hours at home before venturing back outside. I wasn't on the schedule to work, but I wanted to get out of the house. Somehow my life, which seemed okay before the kiss, now seemed empty and lonely.

As I stood inside the doorway of Roy's Bar, I debated on what to do next.

Kandra smiled at me. "You're off. What are you doing here?"

I shrugged. "Just visiting."

She glanced at Ethan, but I refused to follow her stare, though I already knew he was there. It was like I had a homing beacon set for that man.

Kandra might be married to his brother Noah, but I wasn't comfortable with her knowing my true feelings for him. Flirting was one thing, but being head over boots was another.

The place was nearly empty, even though the snow had melted away. The cold weather warned that Old Man Winter would be back, and the ice on the roads was an omen of colder weather to come.

Gypsy patted the seat beside her, and I walked over, relieved to evade Kandra's knowing gaze. She was nice enough, but it was exhausting keeping my guard up all the time. The table before me was scattered with papers, and Gypsy seemed frazzled. "Can I ask for your help?" She peered up at me with pleading eyes.

"Sure." I sat down beside her and waited for her to tell me what she needed.

After a sigh, she began, "My granddaughter, Isla, is supposed to do a school project about family trees, and I'm stumped." Gypsy ruffled through the papers, and I shifted uncomfortably in my seat. Why was she talking to me about family trees? Glancing sideways at Roy, I wondered if something had come out.

He smiled, and I gave him a nervous little wave. The stress of my secret was making me crack around the edges.

"How can I help?" I wanted to understand as quickly as possible why she was asking me questions. As we talked, I watched Ethan walk to the bar. Our gazes locked, and liquid heat filled my belly and spilled over into the rest of me.

Gypsy cleared her throat. "How are things between you two?" Her eyes ticked to Ethan as I turned my attention back to her.

With glasses on, connected by a brightly beaded string around her neck, she could be anyone's grandma. Her usually bright outfits seemed muted today. I took in the deep green sweater and long flowing green and white dress and wondered how she wasn't cold.

"Um, fine?" I didn't know how to answer her question. It wasn't as if Ethan and I saw one another—not exclusively. We made no promises. We hadn't actually been on a date. And I didn't want to make our budding relationship seem like a bigger deal than it was. It was a kiss—a kind of hit and run. I hit him with a kiss and then, feeling silly, ran inside my house.

She stopped moving, all her attention zeroing in on me like a hungry hawk locking on a field mouse. "You know you don't have to hide things from me. It's no one's business but your own, but I'm happy to be here for you to confide in. Everyone needs someone to talk to."

I nodded, mulling over her words. "Thank you for the kind offer. You know, that goes both ways. I'm here if you need someone to talk to as well."

She gestured to the papers on the table. "I know. And here we are. Do you know why it is so difficult for me to help Isla with this project?"

I shook my head. "Isla is a beautiful name, though." I liked the pleasant way it buzzed on my tongue, and the sound had a nice ring to it.

"Thank you. She's a sweet little thing. The apple of her mother's and father's eyes." A deep frown split her forehead in two. "What makes this so much harder is I don't know my father. That whole side of the family tree is blank, and I don't want to disappoint her. It's such a difficult thing to discuss with a child, you know?" Gypsy's shoulders drooped as if life had beaten her down. "How do you tell a child that you don't know your parent because they couldn't be bothered to be a part of your life?"

My throat closed. There was no way she didn't know why I was in Cross Creek. This was too much of a coincidence. I inhaled a few breaths, trying to calm my nerves. "There are online resources that can help you trace your heritage." Everything I'd gone through, everything I'd done leading up to that moment, prepared me to help her with a school project for little Isla. "I can send you some links."

She beamed at me. "You mean it? Can I give you my email address?"

I nodded and took out my phone. My hands shook as I struggled to process that my cover was surely blown. No way my secrets weren't coming out. She rattled off her email address, and I sent her links to the top free family tree services I used and one paid site with better results.

"Thank you." She bounced in her seat like a woman who'd won a prize.

"You're welcome. I'm glad to help." I smiled and put my phone back into my pocket. I could feel Ethan's gaze on me, like a hot caress, and tried to keep my attention on Gypsy. Would she know we kissed from our glances? Could she feel the electricity dancing through the air? I could.

"I assume you had those sites ready because you've used them?" Her hand covered mine, and I studied the point of contact as my chest ached, and my lungs stopped working. How could I answer that without divulging everything?

I nodded. "I also don't know my father," I whispered, hoping my honesty didn't come back to bite me in the butt.

"I know how hard that is." Her kind tone and warm hand on mine helped dull some of the ache washing through me. I had to be very careful not to give away more than that.

"I hope to find him one day, but I don't know if that'll happen. The trail has gone cold." I flashed a smile I didn't feel and stared at the worn, shiny wooden tabletop. It wasn't an all-out lie—the trail had gone cold, but I had a good idea who I was looking for and where he might be. I chanced a quick peek at Roy before turning back to her. "When is this project due?" I asked, trying desperately to steer attention away from me.

"The end of the semester. It's her final project." Gypsy seemed lost once again as she looked over the papers scattered before her. "But I think you've made it a much more doable activity. Maybe we'll both get lucky and find what we're looking for."

"Hope springs eternal." I patted her hand with my free one and stood up. "I'm going to go see how Ethan's doing. Thank you for the lovely chat."

She nodded with a tired smile. "It was my pleasure. Thank you again for the information." Gypsy studied her phone, and I knew she was reading the stuff I'd sent. No doubt she'd get on the site and learn everything she could about herself and her family. I hoped the answers she wanted would be there. Growing up, not knowing was agonizing, and until I found out, there would be a void.

I always likened it to having a hole inside me. I knew something was missing, but I never really knew what. So, I tried to fill the void with different things, hoping something would fit, and I'd feel whole for once. Only, it never happened, and I felt emptier than I did before I started searching. Every dead end chipped at my resolve until I was just about ready to give up, but I needed answers to so many questions.

I couldn't imagine being Gypsy's age and knowing nothing. I wouldn't wish that on an enemy, much less a friend.

I sat down with Ethan, and he turned off his tablet and set it down before gifting me with a smile. It was a gift because he didn't smile that often. Out of the brothers, he was the guarded one.

"How are you?" he asked.

"Good." Warm fuzzy feelings danced over my skin like the

touch of the softest cashmere as I realized he was giving me all of his attention. For once, I didn't have to compete with his work.

I wanted to kiss him again but felt shy around him now. It was as if that kiss changed something between us. Then again, maybe it was all in my head. Perhaps nothing had changed.

"How are you?" I asked.

"I'm good. Did you drive in today?" He planted his elbows on the table and leaned toward me.

"I did. Why?" Was there some reason I shouldn't have been driving?

He nodded toward the decorative windows we worked on together to make look festive. "It's snowing again."

I followed his line of sight and saw the snow falling steadily outside. Maybe that's why no one was coming to the bar. Of course, most people in town drove big trucks like the Lockharts, but maybe they still didn't want to risk the danger. Even big trucks could catch a patch of ice and slide off the road.

"Is that why this place is so dead?" I asked, not expecting him to follow my entire train of thought. It was more of an offhanded question than a serious one, but to my surprise, he responded.

"Yep. In weather like this, the biggest danger isn't the ice or snow; it's the other drivers." He smiled at Kandra as she put a box of pizza in front of him. "Thank you."

She responded warmly and walked away while I stared at him.

Ethan's attention skipped back to me. "Should I follow you home to make sure you get there safely?"

"I don't want your dinner to get cold," I said with a nod at his pizza.

He shrugged. "That's the nice thing about pizza; it's good whether it's hot or cold." With the box in hand, he stood up.

Of course, I agreed with him; everyone knew pizza was good no matter what—especially Roy's pizza. The man knew how to make a good pie.

"I'm happy to follow you home," he said.

The thought thrilled me. "Sure, if you wouldn't mind." At least if he followed me home, I knew I wouldn't end up in a ditch somewhere, and if I did, he'd be there to pull me out again. Moving forward, I needed to plan better or go out less. The weather was only going to get worse the rest of the year. "I don't want to put you out." I followed him to the exit.

"I don't mind at all." He held the door open for me, and we stepped into the bitter winter chill. The snow's crisp scent stung my nose, and my lungs burned as I made my way to my car, still thinking about that kiss and wondering if he was thinking about it too?

"About the other night—" My foot slid out from under me on the slippery concrete, and he caught me as I went down.

Somehow he pulled me into his arms and saved his pizza. "Be careful."

My heart thundered, and I wondered if maybe I was wrong about pursuing him. Perhaps it'd be okay for me to split my focus. I could enjoy his company and fall in love, all while finding the answers I desperately sought.

He was such a good man. What could go wrong?

CHAPTER SIX

ETHAN

I NOTICED Max hesitate at my mailbox and stretch his back with a look of discomfort. Despite the two feet of snow outside, he still made his daily mail trek from house to house. For as many years as I'd known the man, he'd never been one to miss a day of work, though he looked more exhausted than I'd ever seen him.

Opening the door, I called out to him. "Hey, Max, come in and warm up." I already had an electric kettle heating water.

His head whipped around, and I realized he didn't know I'd been watching him. A smile crossed his face, and he meandered up to my sidewalk where I shoveled the snow not an hour before.

"Are you the one keeping everything clear?" he asked with a suspicious stare that told me he knew I was responsible for the clean walkways.

"It's not safe. I don't need anyone breaking a hip on my walk." Despite my stern tone, he clapped me on the back with a hearty chuckle.

"I appreciate the gesture. It's hard to get around this time of year." He gratefully accepted the hot cup of tea I offered. "Thank you." His hands trembled despite his fleecy gloves, and I wanted to offer more.

"My spare key is under the first knob on my railing. Let yourself in anytime to warm up, okay?" I hated the thought of him out in the cold with no real way to get warm. I knew from experience that the older we got, the more the cold hurt. I was only in my thirties and my bones creaked in bad weather.

"Thank you for the generous offer." He seemed impressed as he sipped the hot tea.

"We've got to take care of each other." As the holidays closed in, more and more, they reminded me of my father's lessons. This time of the year had been busy in our household, and not only because we were shoveling sidewalks for all the neighbors. As it was, I knew I had to head out to Ethel and Norman's, the townfolk's favorite septuagenarians, to put chains on their tires soon if my brothers hadn't beat me to it.

He nodded. "You sound like your father."

That statement hit me square in the chest, and I stood there in stunned silence. He glanced up at me with a warm smile. "I mean it. You sound just like Kip."

I sat down in the dining room chair across from him and tried to keep the past from running over me.

"How are things between you and Angie?" Max didn't seem to notice my internal struggle, or he did and ignored it, so I focused on him and his question.

"She kissed me." The words burst out. Nudging my tablet to the side, I studied Max, who blinked as if what I said was the last thing he expected to hear, and he was still trying to process the information.

"Her car slid into a snowdrift, and I pulled her out and towed her home. She wasn't hurt or anything. It wasn't a terrible accident, it just scared her, and she needed help to get home." The flood of words wouldn't stop until I laid everything out there for him to consider.

"Well, that's an interesting development. How do you feel about all of it?" He finished his tea, and I offered another. With a shake of his head, he encouraged me to keep talking.

"Well, I liked the kiss if that's what you're asking." What an odd conversation. One I never expected to have. "It was a surprise. A pleasant surprise, though."

I felt like a teenager again, sitting on my bed and talking to my father about my first crush. Dad's advice was to treat her right—to be a good man with a good heart. Things didn't work out with Cindy because she abused my trust and used me as a shield. Her parents liked my family and liked me, so she'd sneak around with the town's bad boy and tell them she was with me. Despite that, my father's advice stuck with me.

I noticed Max rubbing his side and wondered if he'd injured his back. Maybe he slipped on the ice. What if he'd fallen? That hurt. I knew because I'd done it. Zero stars out of ten. I didn't recommend falling on ice. Though I could see the pain in his eyes, he didn't address the injury.

"Have you talked to her yet? Remember, it's important that you make your expectations clear. Communication is everything." He stood up slowly and stretched before carrying his cup to the sink.

"Don't you dare wash that," I warned.

He glanced over his shoulder.

"My mother would have my hide if she found out my guest washed dishes in my home." It was only kind of a joke. My mother's sense of etiquette at home might be lax, but she was much less forgiving with how we treated others. Like my father, she brought us up to always be kind and good to the people around us even when we didn't want to be, especially if the people in question were cruel to us. "Lead by example," my mother always said.

Max set the cup inside the sink. "I wouldn't want to get you in trouble with your mother."

"Thank you." I breathed a sigh of relief, more for his benefit than anything else. "I haven't had the chance to talk to Angie." Every time we meet up, other things get in the way.

Last night she seemed worried about getting home safely, and I hadn't wanted to keep her out later to have a conversation.

"I'd make it a priority if I were you. Especially since things seem to escalate." Max's fatherly tone brought a slight smile to my face.

"Did you and your wife have these kinds of issues?" It wasn't the most graceful transition, but my curiosity was killing me. What if Max wanted to talk about his past but didn't feel comfortable because everyone avoided the subject? Or, more likely, because no one knew he'd ever been married?

He shook his head. "Not these kinds of issues, no. We were a good fit. We only ever argued about one thing, and I wish I'd taken a stronger stand." His expression softened as he seemed to drift off to another time and place.

It was mind-blowing for me to think one argument could end a marriage. Whatever they argued about must have been a doozy.

What could be such a big deal that things went from good to over with one fight?

"Have you thought more about her flirting? Is it something you can live with?" Max steered the conversation back to Angie and me, but it didn't fool me—I knew he was avoiding talking about his ex-wife.

"It bothers me. I have some trouble trusting that she's interested only in me. What if she's just being nice, like she is to everyone, and there's nothing special about me?" That's what was bothering me. Not so much that I worried she was with someone else; it worried me that she didn't care about me more than anyone else in her life.

"Want to know what I think?" Max asked.

I nodded. Of course, I wanted to know Max's opinion because I trusted him and valued his input.

"I think all this worry is in your head. All your failings, all your insecurities about being picked last, I think that's you." Despite the harsh words, his warm tone and gentle expression took the sting out of what he said.

Was he right?

"Think about it. You hold yourself back, right? What has Angie done to make you honestly think she's interested in someone else?" Max put a hand on my shoulder before sitting back down across from me.

"She took another guy's number, put it in her phone, then went to the town he lives in and refused to let me tag along with her for the trip." Damn, it sounded wrong when I said all those words out loud in that order.

"Where did she go and do you know for sure she went to see

him?" Max didn't sound convinced, despite what seemed like an airtight case to me.

"She went to Silver Springs to supposedly get her hair done, but I'm not sure. I didn't follow her or anything." I wasn't a damn psycho. I was simply a man with a healthy amount of skepticism. "Though ... when I saw her, her hair did smell like a salon." I could be suspicious and logical at the same time.

"You think she met a guy, got his number, and went to visit him the next day? Does that sound like any woman you know?" Max let out a snort. "That doesn't sound like Angie. I know she's a flirt, but, son, she's not a *go home with a guy the day after she meets him* kind of girl. And if her hair smelled like a salon, then maybe you need to accept that she got her hair done, and you're just making up the rest."

He was right. I'd known Angie since she moved to town, and while she was a flirt, that's about all she was. There were no rumors about her hooking up with a string of men. She was mostly a loner like myself.

"Look, you hold yourself back. I see that. Other people see that. I thought you saw that about yourself, but now I worry you don't," he patted my arm, "and that's a damn tragedy."

His words echoed some of what my father had said to me when I was younger, and I sat there stunned.

"I should get back to work because the mail won't deliver itself." He stood up with a big smile and headed for the door. "Think about what I've said, okay?"

I nodded and stood up to see him out the door. There was no way I'd forgo manners simply because he threw me a curveball that glanced off my head.

"Thank you for the tea and for letting me warm up. I appreciate it." He gave me a hug before turning and heading back toward the sidewalk. I watched him go, my mind still reeling.

With a wave at him, I noticed the snow had finally stopped. Peering up into the white skies, I wondered if Angie was safe. I headed back inside and pulled out my phone to send her a text. *Are you okay?*

Cautioning myself not to expect a quick reply, I grabbed my tablet and made my way to my couch. The second I stretched out, my phone chimed.

I am. How are you?

I couldn't hold back a smile. *I'm doing better now that I'm talking to you.* There was no reason to wait. We could have a conversation. Maybe not the big one yet because I couldn't help but feel I needed to build up to that and maybe attach an actual relationship to it. I wasn't sure we were there yet, but I didn't doubt we were close.

Flatterer. I enjoy talking to you too.

I chuckled. I wasn't trying to sweet-talk her. I enjoyed our conversations and knowing she did too was a wonderful feeling. *How is your car holding up in the snow?*

The thought of her driving to and from work made me nervous. I didn't mind coming to her rescue, but I wanted her in a situation where I didn't have to save her in the first place.

Oh, Roy is going to take me to work moving forward.

I sat upright on the couch and stared at her words on my screen. Roy was taking her to work? It was a sweet gesture from the older man, but I had a better idea.

You know, I could start taking you into work and bringing you home. Being between projects like we were meant I was bored more often than not and taking her to and from work was a great excuse to spend time with her. I only wished I thought of it sooner.

She must have had the same idea because her response was nearly instant. *I'd like that. Thank you.*

I liked the idea too. I liked it a lot.

CHAPTER SEVEN

ANGIE

MY PHONE RANG, and I picked it up as I stared at the info I compiled over the last few months. Everything I learned pointed to Roy but getting factual information out of people seemed impossible. No one wanted to talk about themselves or their histories. Did people move to small towns to disappear? Were small towns havens for those looking to start over?

"Hello?" Distracted, I realized I hadn't looked to see who called.

"Hi, Angie." Roy's voice startled me. He stepped out of my thoughts and into reality with a single call. "Kandra called out tonight. Is there any chance you can cover for her?"

I leaned forward, still scanning the papers I printed up as something occurred to me. How had I overlooked it? My father would have certain tells if he were related to me—things no one else would notice but would stand out like a pimple on the tip of a nose to me. I needed to be on the lookout for the tells.

"Sure, what time?" Still distracted, I picked up the family tree

I'd been piecing together. I would find the truth, one way or another. Someone would slip up. My birth father would reveal himself to me. I was sure of that.

"In an hour. I'll come to pick you up." Roy sounded relieved. "Thank you for doing this."

I set the sheet down. "I actually might have a ride. Let me check. That way, you don't have to leave the bar." It was the one issue we hadn't been able to solve, but Cross Creek seemed to be filled with generous people, so getting a ride wasn't a huge concern.

"Let me know." With that, he hung up the phone, and I pulled up my messenger to send Ethan a text.

Unexpected shift, can you take me to Roy's in an hour, please? I waited for a reply and cleaned up the papers scattered on my table.

My phone chimed, and I picked it up. *I'll be there.*

As my heart did a little dance, I typed *thank you* and hit send. When I initially made friends with the Lockhart brothers, I thought they were merely a means to an end. Their family had lived in Cross Creek for a long time, making them a logical choice for information. I was sure they'd be able to help me, whether they knew they were helping me or not, and they did. If I couldn't work with inclusion, I had to work with deduction, and getting the test results back from the Lockharts proved without a shadow of a doubt that we weren't related.

I could've ignored them from that point on, but Ethan was a monkey wrench in everything. As hard as I tried to focus on finding my father, my heart seemed to want something else from that one Lockhart brother. I knew I was stupid. Getting involved with someone wasn't a good idea, and nothing good would come of it when people found out I was here searching for my biological father but had kept it a secret while trying to sneak around to get answers. No one would fault me for that, would they? I mean, someone trying to find their dad doesn't look like a jerk for doing everything in their power to achieve that goal, right? I didn't want anyone to know my mom lied to me all of my life or that I was dumb enough to fall for her BS. I trusted her because trusting your parents should be a given, but I shouldn't have. It made me question everything.

It wasn't as if my goal was to get something from my father. I wasn't looking for someone to pay my bills or nail for past child support, if that was even possible. I wanted to know where I came from, who he was, and if he was sick like me?

Shoving those troubling thoughts aside, I hurried to get ready for work. Maybe today would be the day I learned the truth. Maybe Roy would say something or give some sign that would be proof positive he was my dad.

The sound of Ethan's truck pulling into my drive kicked me into high gear, and I grabbed the last few things I needed, slipped on my shoes, and hurried out the door. The cold hit me like a wall separating the warm indoors from the frozen outside, and my cheeks stung right away. Hurrying along my walkway, I headed to Ethan's truck, opened the door, and climbed into the warmth.

"It's so cold." I shivered and held my hands in front of the heater vent. "Thank you for this."

"You're welcome. I was going to come in to get you, but you bolted out so quickly." The warmth and hint of humor in his voice made my cheeks heat.

"I was ready for you." I pulled on the seat belt and settled into the comfort of his truck as he eased toward the road. "I used to love the snow as a kid. Now, as an adult with responsibilities, it's more of a nuisance."

He glanced sideways at me. "Well, I'm happy to drive you. Maybe you can get back to that childlike sense of wonder and enjoy the snow again."

I stared out the window at the lacy white tree branches.

"Maybe," I said. It was nice not to worry about driving, and the company was good. "How are you doing?"

"Keeping warm, of course. I swear I spend more time shoveling the walk outside my place than anything else." He gave his head a rueful shake, and I couldn't help but notice how handsome he was in the overcast light of the day.

"I'm terrible at shoveling mine. I invited Max in because I felt bad that he had to be out there in the knee-deep snow. I gave him a cup of cocoa, and we chatted about nothing for a while. He's easy to talk to, and I enjoy his company."

Ethan chuckled as he tightened his hands on the wheel and sped up slightly on the main road. "I invited Max in too. Gave him tea, though."

"I bet we're not the only ones. If everyone in town is giving him drinks and feeding him, he's going to resemble Santa by the time the holidays are over." My teasing tone earned a chuckle from Ethan, and I smiled at the thought. Max would make an excellent Santa with his easygoing attitude and kind disposition. I could imagine him inspiring kids and teaching them the meaning of Christmas.

"He's a good guy." Ethan seemed lost in his thoughts, and I nodded. "He's always there when I need someone to talk to."

And it hit me; what if Max had the answers I was looking for? He never talked about other people, but that didn't mean he didn't know everyone's secrets. Cross Creek trusted him, and I knew he was the person everyone went to with their problems. It hadn't occurred to me that his knowledge might hold the missing link to figure out if Roy was my father.

"Cross Creek wouldn't be the same without him." I relaxed as Ethan pulled into Roy's parking lot and came to a careful stop in a nearby spot. "Thank you."

He turned off the truck and turned to me with a smile. "I might as well walk you in and grab a drink."

I nodded, and we headed inside shoulder-to-shoulder. The walkway was clear of snow, and the warm golden glow of lights welcomed us out of the cold. Inside, warmth enveloped me like a hug, and I realized Roy had turned on holiday music.

"I love the holidays." He boomed as we walked inside. People smiled at him as he continued. "It's cold outside but warm in here, where people come to gather," He gestured at the tables of people sitting together, and some lifted their glasses to him, some smiled, and Gypsy sighed, watching him with adoration. "There's a sense that everything is wonderful. Thank you for coming in," he said as I walked up to him.

"No worries. Is Kandra all right?" I worried about her.

"She said she is." Roy ushered me back, and I looked over orders. The place was half-full of familiar faces. Roy had expanded the menu to include a few other dishes, turning the place from pizza and beer to more family-friendly dishes like salads and fresh-made bread bowls for his soups and stews.

"I love the changes." I glanced at him as Ethan took a seat.

Roy smiled from ear to ear. "I wanted to try something different this year and make this a place where families could gather for more than a pizza. If it goes well, I might consider transitioning from a bar and pizza joint to a full-blown restaurant."

He leaned in close as if to tell me a secret. "And if that happens, I'll need a lot more help. I've already prepped everything, but I'll gladly teach you my family recipes."

My head reeled, and I stared at him. Was I about to learn family recipes from the man I thought was my father? Conflicted and unsure how to feel, Ethan's voice from the bar saved me. "Hey, I like the new additions. Is the cheddar broccoli soup available in the garlic bread bowl?"

"Certainly," Roy said, turning his attention to Ethan and leaving me locked in place.

"I'd like that and a beer, please." Ethan sat down, and Roy beamed at me.

"Tell me about your favorite traditions growing up?" I asked Roy, trying to wrap my head around the thought that these might be traditions I could continue. Roy was right about the holiday season; I couldn't get the idea of family out of my head.

"We used to fill each other's stockings. My parents would give us a spending limit and tell us to get something nice for everyone, and we'd try to outdo one another by getting the best small stocking stuffers. My mother always won." Roy shook his head, his eyes sparkling.

"I love that." It was such a sweet idea, one that never would have occurred to me. "Did you grow up here in Cross Creek?"

Roy nodded. "I did, but moved to Silver Springs for a while, and wound up moving back. Something about this town, you know?"

I nodded my head. What he said fit with the data I had but didn't give me any additional answers. "I get it. I love it here. Can't imagine living anywhere else." Would I move once I discovered the truth? Maybe. However, there was something about this town that drew me in. I loved Cross Creek and the people that lived there.

"I love that tradition," Ethan said to Roy.

I glanced sideways at him as Roy grinned.

"Did your family have the same tradition?" Roy asked Ethan.

"My mom and dad used to fill ours, but they were sparse with the candy and sugary treats," Ethan said. "They'd get us a new book, a hand-written coupon for an activity, a keepsake from a special event, and just a little candy." His wistful expression brought a smile to my lips. "I remember when they gifted me the plaque for the first-ever design I did."

"I bet you still have that," Roy said with an approving nod.

"I do," Ethan lit up with his response, and I struggled against that feeling of being left out.

I loved their stories, but sadness nagged at me as well. My mother was never one for celebrations. I didn't have fun, loving, incredible memories of holidays spent with family like Roy and Ethan did. Holidays were simply another day growing up in my house.

I smiled at Ethan. "I'll get your order started now."

CHAPTER EIGHT

ETHAN

"YOU WILL INVITE HER." My mom said, not taking no for an answer as we stood in her kitchen, surrounded by my brothers as they continued to cook.

"Yeah, Ethan, invite her." Quinn's eyes sparkled as he mixed cornstarch in cool water to integrate into the broth to make gravy. Sunday afternoon never seemed this dangerous. I could tell Quinn to go to hell, but if Mom wanted me to invite her, then I had no choice.

"Okay, okay." I pulled out my phone under my mother's watchful eye and thumbed a text to Angie. *Hey, you're invited to family dinner. I can pick you up if you want to come.*

Honestly, I wasn't sure if I hoped she'd say yes or no. While I wanted the time with her, I wasn't sure I wanted to subject her to the family dinner where my brothers would feel justified in asking her any question that came to mind.

I turned the phone around to show mom. "See? I texted her."

Quinn grabbed the phone, stared hard at it, then nodded. "Can confirm. He sent it to her."

I glared at him for a second before noticing the twinkle in mom's eyes. "I don't know why young people don't just call one another," she said.

"Texts are easier," Quinn spoke up as if he had any idea on how relationships worked. "And rejection stings less and isn't as awkward via text."

"Since when do you know anything about dating?" Bayden shoulder checked Quinn as he walked back to his gravy-making, an action that would've been far messier if Quinn still had the cornstarch in hand.

Quinn lifted his shoulders. "Maybe you don't know everything about me." With his focus on the broth, he added to his cornstarch mix and didn't seem to notice everyone in the room stop what they were doing to stare at him.

"Did you meet someone?" I asked, wondering who'd put up with Quinn's antics. He still seemed too young to date anyone, though I knew he was a grown-ass man.

Quinn glanced up as if suddenly aware of all of us. "*Pfft*. Like I'd tell you guys. All of you complicate everything. Besides, I'm more of a once burned, twice shy guy." And he went back to his gravy, ignoring us as we stared.

Mom's smile grew, and I shrugged at her. He had a point; family made things more complicated. If Bayden hadn't been pretending with Angie to make me jealous, then Angie and I would likely be together by now. I had no idea how they all messed with each other's relationships, but I didn't doubt it happened. Still, since when was Quinn the one in the know about anything?

My phone vibrated, and all attention leaped back to me as I checked the message. *I'd love to come. I'll be ready in ten.*

Angie was coming to the family dinner. I scanned the hopeful, questioning faces of my family and noticed Mom's expectant expression. I still wasn't sure how serious things would become, but it didn't stop my mom from wishing. "She said she'd love to join us, but I have to go pick her up."

Noah glanced at Kandra, who gave him a slight smile as she stepped into the kitchen. "Can I help?" she asked softly.

"Finally, we're getting rid of you," Quinn said, clapping me on the shoulder. "Go pick up your girlfriend."

I focused on the exchange between Kandra and Noah. "No," Noah said. "Go sit; I've got this." She gave him a sweet smile and left the kitchen, no doubt to sit with Kip. Miranda hadn't shown up yet because she had some work to do before she could get away.

With a nod at Mom, I grabbed my keys and jacket and headed into the snow. Within fifteen minutes, I was at Angie's house, and she bolted out the same way she had the previous Thursday when I took her to work.

She got into the truck and stared at me a second before offering a breathless, "Hi."

"Hello." She was beautiful in her black leggings and long, plum-colored sweater. There was something wholesome and innocent about her that drove me wild. The girl-next-door look extended to the light touch of makeup she added to accentuate her eyes and her somewhat messy bun.

The urge to lean in and kiss her filled me, but I shrugged the feeling off and put the truck in gear instead. My family was waiting, and I had a feeling if I started kissing her, I wouldn't make it back to Mom's.

She pulled on her seat belt, and when I heard it click, I drove.

"Should I have brought something?" she asked, sounding worried.

I shook my head. "We're pretty informal. We do this more for my mom than anything, though I think we all like the time together."

"I bet that annoys your mom, the thought that everyone's just doing it for her." As she stared out the window, I realized how my words sounded.

"I didn't mean it like that. I meant we cook for her because we never wanted her to be stuck in the kitchen while everyone else sat and enjoyed themselves. We do the cooking. Mostly it means we stand in the kitchen and BS until the food is ready, then we move to the dining room and BS while eating." I chuckled, well aware she stopped looking at the snow to study me.

"What?" I asked, glancing sideways at her.

"That's sweet," she said in a surprised voice. "I love that you make food for your mom to keep her from missing out on family time."

I lifted my shoulders. "We're family, and everybody chips in when they can."

"Well, now I wish I'd brought something." She went back to staring out her window.

"Next time," I said, not expecting her to agree. To my surprise, she responded instantly.

"Absolutely. Do you guys plan what you're making in advance?" This time, she turned around in her seat as much as possible to focus on me.

I nodded. "Usually. I'll make sure we include you in the conversation for next week." I pulled into the driveway and killed the engine. Was it prudent to warn her about what she'd walk into? Or should I let her experience this meal organically? Would she be able to handle all of them? This would be a cornerstone in our budding relationship. If she hated family dinners, there was no way we could make things work between us.

"Do I look okay?" she asked, her wide eyes worried.

"You're beautiful." I meant the words, and her cheeks went pink as she gave a tiny smile that made my heart flip. As I opened my door, I realized things were about to get interesting. Meeting my family was like entering a quick-fire game show.

Side by side, we moved toward the front door, and her hand slipped into mine. Our fingers laced together, and I knew she was uneasy. I felt like I was bringing home my first real girlfriend with all the nerves, buzzing gut, dry mouth, and thundering pulse that came with that.

Mom met us at the door and pulled Angie into a hug, welcoming her. Over Angie's shoulder, she winked at me, showing that she was pleased. I could only hope she didn't have something up her sleeve.

In the kitchen, my brothers were putting the finishing touches on dinner, and Angie lifted her nose in the air. "It smells great in here, guys."

Everyone descended on her, pulling her into hugs, asking her if she was out of her mind wasting her time on me, and otherwise welcoming her to the family. My mother quickly whisked her into the dining room, and I stood rooted in place and torn between staying here or following them.

Quinn dropped a hand on my shoulder. "Go. We've got this

covered." He gave me a quick nod, and I thanked him before following Mom and Angie to the dining room.

Mom, Angie, and Kandra talked while Angie held Kip in her arms. I stopped, stunned at the sight of her with a baby and the sweet, thrilled expression on her face as she smiled down at the infant.

In the kitchen, a commotion started, and Miranda's voice echoed through the room. With everyone present, dinner could officially begin. As the food came out of the kitchen and the baby got settled into his swing, conversations carried on, and laughter made the space brighter.

"When are you and this loser going to tie the knot?" Quinn put his boat of gravy on the table and elbowed Angie before gesturing at me.

Noah chuckled, and Bayden lifted both shoulders as if he didn't know how to help me.

"You're ahead of yourself, Quinn. By the way, how is your girl? Oh, that's right, you don't have one. Shall we find you one, or do you have it under control?" Angie stared at him with an innocent look on her face, and he instantly clammed up, glared at all of us, and turned red.

"Let it be." With that, he disappeared into the kitchen so fast I wondered if he discovered the secret of teleportation. My brothers and I all glanced at one another and laughed.

I didn't have to worry about Angie handling herself. She put Quinn right in his place.

"Wow, you know how to handle him." Bayden sounded impressed as Miranda wrapped her arms around his shoulder and planted a kiss on his cheek. He smiled at his beloved and planted a quick kiss on her lips.

Angie laughed. "Working at the bar has its perks," she said with a broad smile. "I have to deal with troublemakers all the time. Hope I didn't overstep."

"Oh no. Quinn's reaction says he likes you, otherwise, he would have bitten your head off." Miranda gave Angie a quick shoulder hug.

I couldn't help but stare at Angie. I thought my brothers would chew her up and spit her out, but I'd never seen someone shut Quinn down as quickly as she had. Maybe I should've been more worried for my brothers.

"It's nice to have you here." Mom smiled.

"Thank you for inviting me," Angie said, threading her fingers through mine once more. We sat side by side at the table, and again I was amazed by Angie's humor, grace, and wit. Still, there was something sad in her eyes I hadn't noticed before. She fit right in at the table with the family, yet she seemed to believe she didn't belong. I could see in her tight smile that she wasn't truly letting loose despite her comment to Quinn.

Angie continued to smile at me as the conversation ensued. "Did he tell you how he saved my life while I was decorating Roy's?" She patted my hand as my brothers, their significant others, and my mother filled their plates.

"No, he didn't." Mom's glance told me she'd have choice words for me for not telling her this juicy story.

Quinn rejoined the group and elbowed me, nearly knocking my plate from my hand while I piled ham onto it. I wanted to smack him off his seat as he chuckled evilly beside me. Angie lit up as she told the story. I offered her mashed potatoes, and Mom passed her the gravy.

"I was on the ladder and just stretching to hang the lights, and *poof,* he appeared at the right moment to grab me as the ladder slid and fell. It was like a Hallmark Christmas Movie without the sappy stuff that makes me want to gag, vomit, and stab myself in the eye."

Miranda laughed, and Kandra giggled while the guys glanced from me to Angie, knowing expressions on their faces. I noticed Noah and Kandra murmuring and saw my opening to turn the attention away from us to them.

"Everything okay?" They'd been acting strange all day.

Noah didn't look at me or anyone else; instead, he studied Kandra as if silently offering her strength. Kandra nodded, sighed, and apologized to Angie for running over her story.

Angie graciously nodded and said, "No worries."

Kandra smiled and scanned the faces around the table as Noah studied her. "We're pregnant again."

CHAPTER NINE

ANGIE

ETHAN WALKED me to my front door and stopped. Turning to him, I couldn't help but notice the warmth in his eyes as the cold dug into my skin like icy claws. Without overthinking it, I opened the door and pulled him inside.

"It's way too cold out there," I said with a smile as we stood in the entryway. "I also wanted to thank you for including me." I enjoyed myself, even though the sadness of never having had that kind of loving relationship with my family sunk in. I was certainly jealous of the love they all shared, though I was happy for him, and it meant a lot that they welcomed me.

"Of course. We should've invited you sooner." He smiled down at me as his cologne filled my nose and my belly heated up. It was the first time he'd been in my home. The first time I'd had any man in my house. The oddly intimate gesture didn't bother me as it should have. My home was my castle, and it guarded my secrets.

"I don't think I was ready before," I said honestly. Before I could stop myself, I lifted onto my tiptoes and pressed my lips to his in a chaste *thank you* kiss.

His arms slipped around me, powerful and protective, and my heart turned to pudding. I was kidding myself if I tried to say I didn't like Ethan. Still, I knew better than to get attached because I wasn't even sure if I'd stick around once my mission was complete.

I also wasn't sure I'd be able to search for my father if I dedicated all my time to Ethan. I knew I was the type of person that once I was in a relationship, I was all in. It was hard for me to focus on more than one thing at a time, which always burned me.

"Are you okay?" he asked softly, pressing his forehead to mine as he spoke. His breath on my lips had my pulse racing.

"I am, but I don't think this is a good idea." I might as well be honest. "When I date, I'm in one hundred percent. There's nothing casual about my commitment."

"I'm not into casual relationships either." His answer didn't reassure me because I didn't think he understood exactly what I meant. Still, being in his arms was wonderful, and I didn't want to stop. His lips touched mine, and I felt my walls tumbling down. I fought hard to stay strong, yet here he was, stripping my defenses as if they were nothing.

I wound my arms around his neck and clung to him. When his tongue touched my lower lip, I instinctively opened for him, but he cut the kiss short. "I want things between us to be serious, Angie." I could hear something in his voice like a question, but I wasn't sure what it was.

"Me too. I like you. I always have, and it's always been you." I kissed him and tingling excitement settled low in my belly, and as I deepened the kiss, I needed more of him.

I was breathless when I broke away. "Stay with me tonight," I whispered, unable to speak louder, afraid he'd say no.

My gut told me I was stupid, but my heart wanted this. Didn't I deserve love too?

He nodded. "Okay." I kissed him again before taking his hand and leading him through the living room and down the hallway toward my bedroom. My home was much nicer than I should've been able to afford on a server's salary, and I wondered if he'd notice.

"You have a nice place."

Yep, he noticed. "Thank you." I didn't want to tell him I was a trust fund baby, thanks to a generous aunt. She was the only living relative that gave a damn about me, and we still weren't close. I didn't want to think about sad family stuff, though. I vowed to focus on this man and how he made me feel in this moment.

At the foot of my bed, I pulled off my shirt and let it fall to the floor. His gaze locked on mine, and I lifted my chin in a silent dare for him to do the same.

With a wicked sparkle in his eye, he pulled off his shirt, then stepped in close to pull me into his arms.

His lips touched my neck, and then his teeth scraped my ear, causing heat to flood my body. Excitement battled with logic as my brain warned me of the huge mistake I was making, but my heart and body demanded more. This was my moment, and I was taking it.

Ethan made me feel good, and I wanted what he offered, so I shoved aside all thoughts of why I shouldn't be here.

"I've liked you for a long time," I admitted as he deftly removed the rest of my clothes. "I'm sorry for being stupid and trying to use your brother to make you jealous. That was immature."

He flashed me a devilish grin. "It worked, though." As our skin met, I realized I'd been craving him and dug my fingertips into his back, needing him closer.

"But there's a right way and a wrong way to do things," I whispered. I made a mistake, and I'd own up to it.

He pulled away long enough to slip on protection, and I breathed a sigh of relief that he was responsible because I wasn't on the pill. There was no need to be since my love life was as barren as the Sahara.

He laid me back on the bed and lowered his body over mine. I arched my back into him, loving the way he pressed himself to me. We fit together perfectly. Heart to heart, we met for a quick kiss.

"I'm just glad we're finally figuring things out," he whispered. "I worried we never would. I've wanted you for far too long to stop now."

I also worried about that, but as I stared into his eyes and ran a hand along the back of his neck, I couldn't believe we were finally in the right spot at the right moment. "Same for me." I pulled him in for another kiss, loving how our body heat mingled, and I focused on the warmth and pleasure of his movements. The thrill of the day hadn't worn off, and the feeling of belonging continued each minute I was in his arms.

As the length of him filled me, I exhaled. "I've wanted this, wanted you, since I met you, Ethan."

He glanced into my eyes and let out a growl.

My heart pounded harder, like a jackhammer against concrete chipping away at the loneliness. For a moment, I could imagine a life with Ethan. I could picture us having kids of our own, a house with a picket fence, and a dog. The thought, alien as it was because I never considered having a family, much less marrying someone, filled me with sadness. Kids would never be in the cards for me—it was far too risky. And a man like Ethan, who was brought up in a close-knit family, probably wouldn't want a woman who couldn't give him his own. It wasn't that I couldn't get pregnant. I could, but it wasn't wise or responsible.

"Am I hurting you?" he asked, hesitating and glancing down at me with an expression that said the last thing he wanted to do was hurt me. That bit of information made my heart dance.

I shook my head, trying to ignore the tears that trickled from the corners of my eyes to my ears. "I'm okay. Happy tears. I swear I'm not crazy." Maybe I was a little crazy.

"It's okay if you're crazy," he said, nuzzling into my neck like there was nowhere he'd rather be. His lips and tongue teased and tickled my skin, driving me up the wall as I tried to push all sad thoughts about the future I couldn't have out of my mind.

Ethan didn't know everything that left me feeling guilty and upset with myself, but I was determined to enjoy our time together. I wouldn't let anything hold me back from being in the moment with him. "Please don't stop," I whispered, holding on to him as tightly as I could.

"I won't unless you want me to," he responded, his teeth scraping my shoulder. Goosebumps raced down my arms and across my chest, and I squeezed my eyes closed. With every motion, he drove my body closer to release, and I wondered how long we could be happy before everything fell apart. In my experience, nothing lasted forever.

We moved as if made for one another, and I tried to keep the tears and sad thoughts at bay.

"You're amazing," he breathed, kissing my forehead, the corner of my mouth, and then my lips. "I don't want to stop. I'm not sure I'd be able to." His gaze, serious and sexy, met mine. "I hope you mean you want things to be serious."

"I do," I whispered. I wanted that more than anything.

Every motion, every glance, every kiss, every time his teeth grazed my skin made me crave more. Ethan made me realize that every other lover I had before wasn't right for me. He drew every ounce of pleasure from each motion and left me aching, yearning, and desperate for more, and then he gave me more until my body was replete but well-satisfied.

If I had known this was how it was supposed to be—how things were supposed to feel—I would've lived a different life from the start. "I'm glad you brought me home, and that you came in." I was grateful for everything that led up to this moment.

"Me too," he whispered, kissing my eyelids and moving to my lips.

I wasn't the type to think things happened for a reason, but call it fate, destiny, or sheer luck—something brought us together. As pleasure overtook me and my vision went white, I imagined this being our reality forever. Maybe he never had to find out my reason for being here, or the health issues I painstakingly hid from everyone. Perhaps we could be happy together. But as my vision cleared, I knew better. This was the only moment I had, and it might be the last. People like me didn't get to wish for more.

Warmth filled me as he held me close. His lips met mine, and everything felt right in the world. We shifted as he rolled onto his side, breaking the kiss with a regretful growl.

"I'll be right back," he said, looking me in the eyes and rubbing the tip of his nose against mine. "You better be here when I get back."

I smiled at him, and he kissed me once more before slipping out of the room. I stared up at the ceiling, wondering what would happen next. I knew what I *wanted* to happen next; I wanted him and me to be together in a serious relationship. The problem was that he didn't know why I was in town, and that felt dishonest. Before being intimate with him, I didn't think I owed anyone answers about what I was doing. Now, with some semi-serious promises being made between us, I worried it was my obligation to tell him everything, but I knew my truths would make him mad.

"You're looking pretty intense," he said, standing in the doorway before walking into the room. As he crawled into bed beside me, I rolled onto my side and propped my head up to smile at him.

"I can't believe how lucky I am," I said, thinking it was a good idea to change the subject, "I'm blessed that you're here and staying the night with me."

He grinned like a teenager. "I think I'm the lucky one." He leaned in and pressed another kiss to my lips. I wondered if I'd get any sleep because he was waking up my desire again, and as he said, he wanted me for far too long to stop now.

"Maybe we're both lucky." Looking beyond him to the window, I saw the snow outside continue to fall, cocooning us into our little fantasyland of love, warmth, and joy.

CHAPTER TEN

ETHAN

I WOKE up curled into her with an arm over her ribs, and her body pressed tightly to mine. The house seemed cooler than I expected, but it was warm under the covers. Last night had been amazing and made me think I was the luckiest man alive.

As she slumbered, I glanced out her bedroom window at the snow falling in fat white flakes and wondered how deep it had gotten. The forecast had called for a few inches overnight, so I focused on snuggling Angie's warm naked body.

Being in her home filled me with peace. The sweet scent of lavender and vanilla permeated the space, and her elegant style reminded me of home. Even though she chose brighter colors, whites, and light grays, and I chose charcoals, I still thought our tastes aligned reasonably well.

My grip tightened on her, and she stirred before her breathing deepened once more. I slipped out of bed and headed for the bathroom. The medicine cabinet door was open a few inches, and I noticed orange pill bottles with their stark white lids and labels. It didn't feel right to pry, but I couldn't help but swing the door open a few more inches to get a look at the medications. Not recognizing any of them, I closed the door, did my business, and washed my hands.

Why did she need to take multiple medications a day? I didn't have the right to pry, and I worried I had less right to ask questions about things I discovered while snooping around.

I considered climbing into the shower with my troubling thoughts but headed back into her room instead. Seeing she was still asleep, and worried about waking her, I changed my mind and went right back to the shower.

The neat little room invited me in with clean towels and washcloths, but I was craving the hot water. I also hoped she'd wake and join me, but at the least, I needed to rinse last night's sweat from my skin.

Under the slick, hot needles of water, I pressed my palms to the white tiles and wondered what was next. We kind of made promises to one another, and I liked the thought of us being together in a serious relationship. Max's words repeatedly echoed in my mind that I had no right to expect her to change for me, but if I were her man, I would want her to stop flirting. We needed to have a discussion about our expectations, and the more we put it off, the worse things could become.

I finished up my shower, got out, and dried off. I wished she'd woken up to share the time with me, but apparently, she was still worn out from last night. I didn't want to disturb her, but the thought of spending time with her excited me.

Dressed and considerably cleaner, I snuck into the room to grab my phone before walking into the living room to peek out the window. The snow had deepened—a lot. As I stared at the fast falling flakes, I had a feeling there was no leaving.

Turning on the TV and switching it to the news, I listened to the report about a mini-blizzard with a sinking heart. There was a good chance we'd wind up snowed in and stuck together. I could shovel snow, sure, but not all the way home, and the one guy that could be counted on to plow the roads wouldn't be able to keep up with blizzard conditions.

I called my brothers. "Hey, I'm at Angie's. I might need help to get out."

Noah spoke first. "No plow for my truck, brother."

Quinn was next. "Yeah, it's a no, dude. Have fun while you can."

Bayden stayed quiet a moment. "Well, I'm glad you two are getting more serious, but you need this time. Sorry, I can't help."

When I hung up, I stared at my phone. They ditched me.

It made sense because we didn't have truck plows, but I expected them to offer more support. Instead, they sounded glad I was stuck with Angie. We'd be snowed in together until Wednesday at the earliest. I braved the snow and grabbed my tablet from my truck before hurrying back into the house. Warm and fuzzy inside, I opened up some work while waiting for her to wake up.

With the TV still on and muted, I settled in, feeling warmer and more at home than I had in longer than I could remember. I wasn't sure how much time had passed when the back of my neck prickled, and I glanced up and caught her watching me.

"On your tablet already? Seriously?" Despite the teasing tone of her voice, something in me whispered she wasn't joking.

I set work aside and took in her white cotton T-shirt and little white booty shorts that did dangerous things to my blood pressure. "I didn't want to wake you." Offering her a smile, I watched her features soften. "Good morning."

"Good morning to you," she said. "Are you hungry?"

She had no idea what I was thinking, and it had nothing to do with food. "That depends. Are you on the menu?" I stood up and moved toward her, noticing the excitement in her eyes as she took a step back.

"Absolutely not. I need breakfast." With that, she sailed into the kitchen, leaving me staring at her backside before following her. She rummaged through the fridge and grabbed blackberry jam and a carton of milk.

"Breakfast of champions," she said, pulling an English muffin from the bag and putting it in the toaster. "Please help yourself to whatever." She gestured toward the fridge before getting a pot of coffee brewing.

"I'll have what you're having," I said, and she put in a second muffin. "We're going to be trapped for a couple of days."

Her hands went still for a moment, then she turned to me, her smile frozen on her face. "I'm sorry, what?"

"We're snowed in." I gestured to the TV, and she walked over, picked up the remote, and turned the sound back on. As she watched the news report, an uneasy feeling swept through me. She seemed less than pleased we'd be stuck together—not the response I expected. Was I missing something?

The English muffins popped up, and I walked over and put them on the plates she'd set on the counter. Covering them both with butter and jam, I then poured coffee into two mugs and added milk to hers before putting it away. I moved everything to her chic white table. She wandered back in with a stunned look on her face.

"Are you okay?" I asked, realizing she looked oddly pale.

"Yeah," she said, but she didn't seem fully present. She appeared to be panicking and trapped in her thoughts with no way out. We sat together at the table, but no matter how hard I tried to engage her in conversation, she seemed totally shut down.

"I'm happy to be here with you," I said.

She smiled absently in my direction before continuing to chew.

I studied her as I took a sip of coffee. The snow outside reminded me that the holidays were right around the corner. I was going to have a significant other for Christmas for the first time in a long time. "My family does a big celebration for Christmas. Mom will also want all of us there to decorate the tree." I hoped that would pull her out of her thoughts. Yesterday she seemed so thrilled to be part of the family activities but today seemed different.

"That sounds nice," she said, taking another bite.

She was completely checked out of our conversation. What had I missed?

"Are you stressed about being snowed in?" I asked.

She glanced at me, hesitated, then nodded while swallowing hard.

"Do you want me to leave?" If I was the problem, I'd figure out how to get out of here and let her be.

She shook her head no, but that didn't comfort me. Was she simply being polite? It wasn't a positive response, more like an automatic one. At least, that's what it looked like.

I wasn't the only one that sucked at communication; she wasn't exactly a pro at it either.

"Let's not focus on the snow, but enjoy our time together," I suggested.

With that, she finally seemed to come around a little. A smile tugged at the corners of her lips, and she gave a slight nod. "I'd like that."

"Tell me about your holiday traditions growing up." At the bar, she asked Roy about his, and he and I had shared, but she hadn't said a word about hers.

She nearly choked on her bite. "Next question, please." She took a sip of coffee without looking at me and set the mug down beside her plate.

"Really?" I asked.

Her gaze ticked to mine. "I didn't have holiday traditions. My mom wasn't much of a celebratory person." The sadness I noticed the previous day in her eyes came back with a vengeance, and I wished I hadn't asked.

Taken aback, I studied her for a moment. "I'm sorry. I didn't mean to dig at painful memories." Well, I was screwing things up.

She shook her head. "You didn't know."

I reached out and put my hand over hers. "I am sorry."

She glanced at me, her eyes welling with tears. She nodded, and I had a feeling she couldn't speak if she wanted to.

"You're always welcome to join us for the holidays. In fact, I'm sure you'll be expected to come. Nobody should spend them alone."

"Thank you," she said. "I appreciate that."

She didn't have to thank me. Not only was it the right thing to do, but I also wouldn't want to spend Christmas without her.

I wanted to ask her about the medications, but I didn't want to admit I'd been sneaking around her cabinets.

My tablet made a noise, and I knew the battery was low. "It's almost out of power." It used the same charger as my phone, which was in her bedroom. "I'll be right back." She nodded, and I headed into her room to grab the cord. As I was about to leave, a note on her bedside table jumped out at me.

On it were several names of the men around town. More than half the list had lines drawn through them. What the hell was I staring at? I picked it up as my blood heated. As I read through the list, it rose to a boil. There could've been an innocent explanation, but I couldn't think of one.

I took the note out and slapped it down on the table in front of her. She jolted, a stunned look in her eyes as she stared at me, then glanced at the paper. The last bit of color drained from her features, leaving her looking sickly and terrified. If I didn't know better, I'd be worried she was about to pass out.

"What's this?" I was feeling strangely betrayed and more pissed that she wasn't laughing this off and telling me what the list meant.

Instead, she shook her head as if refusing to answer or unable to believe I was confronting her about it.

If she didn't want to talk, I'd make guesses instead. "Fine, don't tell me, but nod if I'm right. You're in Cross Creek looking for—"

"Ethan, don't." She sounded exhausted, but I couldn't let it go.

"Tell me what it means." Roy's name wasn't crossed out. I could see Max's name, Norman's name … every male in town past a certain age was on the list. Some had a line through them, like Norman. "What are you looking for?"

She shook her head. "Nothing."

I picked it up and waved it in front of her face. "It looks like a damn hit list, Angie. If I hadn't seen Norman yesterday, I'd be inclined to call Miranda and see if everyone crossed out is okay." I scanned the list further, and my heart sank. I glared up at her, then glanced at the names again, unable to believe my eyes.

I spoke through clenched teeth, silently daring her to lie to me. "Angie, why is my father's name crossed out on this list?"

CHAPTER ELEVEN

ANGIE

I STARED at him as he stood over where I sat at the table, unsure what to say before lowering my gaze to my partially eaten breakfast. My stomach ached, and I pressed my hand to the spot as if pressure would ease up the discomfort. The pain and heaviness only intensified, leaving my mouth watering as if throwing up would be the next step.

"It's not a hit list," I said as saliva filled my mouth and threatened to choke me. The world tilted to one side, and I ground my teeth and balled my fists, unwilling to pass out right there in front of him.

"What is it then?" His stilted, quiet tone promised danger, but I had no answers. At least none I could share.

"A list of names." As I continued to put him off, my mind reeled, searching for answers that would satisfy him without making me sound like a crazy person.

I should've never invited him over. That stupid, irresponsible decision would haunt me forever. Taking a sip of coffee, I wished

I'd turned up the heat. My chilled fingers trembled, and a shiver started deep in my core before working its way out. Tears stung my eyes as I realized my time was up. My secrets were barreling forward like a train without brakes.

"This isn't a joke, Angie." His voice was deadly, like six feet under scary.

I nodded. "I'm not messing around." The smell of coffee tickled my nose as the sharp bite of snow outside crept into my senses despite the room's 68-degree temperature. I turned away because I couldn't look at him.

Instead, I fiddled with my jam-coated, half-eaten English muffin. Shoving it along the plate, smudging a bit of jam on the edge of the white porcelain.

"You're stalling, so why won't you just answer the question?" His clothes rustled as he shifted, and I knew he'd crossed his arms without looking at him.

The tension in the air was thick and sat heavy in my chest, causing my lungs to constrict and my gut to ache. As my heart pounded, the sensation of faintness grew and the edges of my vision blurred. "You know how I told you my mother wasn't much for celebrations?" I sucked in a deep breath, then slowly let it out, praying the action would help settle my nerves. I peeked up at him.

"Yes." His voice softened, but his stance stayed rigid.

Looking at him was a mistake; anger resonated through his features and his narrowed eyes told me what he thought. Those beautiful eyes screamed LIAR! and YOU'RE AN AWFUL PERSON. The kicker was, he might be right.

I struggled against rising tears. "She, uh," I tipped my head back toward the ceiling to keep the tears from spilling. My voice warbled dangerously. "She wasn't a sincere person, either."

He stayed quiet, but the tilt of his head and the question in his eyes told me to continue.

"She told me my dad died in the war." My chest compressed, sending pain rippling through me. I leaned forward, putting my elbows on the table and staring at the crumbs dotting the plate before me. "She said he was Native American and claimed I was related to royalty, like somehow I was the tribal chief's cherished offspring. She lied about everything."

I couldn't believe the words spilling from my lips. Saying them out loud made me sound as crazy as it seemed. Was the story planted to give a fatherless girl a fairy tale? It all seemed so ridiculous now. How naïve I'd been to hope, want, and believe anything she said. I gestured to the chair. "Please sit down. You're making me nervous." I didn't like how he stood over me like a bear about to attack. I knew he wouldn't hurt me, but that didn't mean I liked his intimidation technique, either.

After a moment of hesitation, he lowered himself into the seat opposite me, leaned back, stretched his legs out, and crossed his arms. Despite his obvious foul mood, I breathed a sigh of relief. "Thank you."

We both remained silent for a few heartbeats, then I cleared my throat and searched for the next words to say. "I never knew the truth. So, I sought it out myself, and I found out my dad didn't die in a war, nor do I have a drop of Native American blood in my veins." I sighed. "Maybe she didn't know who he was. Whatever the truth may be, I've been searching for him."

"What does this have to do with my father's name on your list?" His words came out like the growl of a rabid dog. I wrapped my arms around myself as my entire body shook. Rather than succumb to the iciness in the air, I stood and headed to the thermostat to crank up the heat.

Turning back to Ethan, my heart fractured at his cold, hard glare. Had I ruined everything between us? Surely, that couldn't be. Once I explained, we could go back to normal. I was certain of it. Ethan was levelheaded and a good man. "I traced my father through my mom's movements back to this town, but I don't know who he is, exactly." I shook my head, not ready to get into the complicated details. "The list is of every man that might be my father. I ruled Kip out because …" I hung my head. "I stole a hair from you at the bar a while back and had it DNA tested."

"You what?" He yelled. "How could you?"

"I was desperate for answers. Besides, I liked you and there was no way I'd ever get intimate with someone if there was a chance we were related."

"That's so wrong. Unforgivable." He grabbed for the list, but I swiped it from the table. "What did you find out?" There was such a chill to his voice I was certain the temperature in the room dropped ten degrees.

"Ethan, we're not related. I mean … I made love to you." I stopped short at my choice of words. We had sex, and to me it felt like love. But the fury in his eyes said it was something else—a big mistake.

He pointed to the paper in my hand. "But he's still on the list."

"He was still on the list, just in case." I returned to my seat, but I couldn't help that fight-or-flight response that kept me perched on the edge.

"Just in case what?" Ethan's rage had me holding my breath.

"I wanted to make sure, so I collected more samples from your brothers, but the results of those came back negative too. That's why I crossed him off—I knew he wasn't my father."

He tossed a nearby pen at me. "Take him off. He never should've been on there in the first place."

I scribbled out his name so it wasn't legible.

"Nobody's perfect, Ethan. Your parents have secrets too." I reached out to touch his arm, but he jerked back.

"Not those kinds of secrets." His distasteful stare stung like a poison arrow pricking my chest, but I refused to let him break me. "And my family wouldn't underhandedly steal DNA samples for their benefit."

"You'll never know because you know who your parents are." I made bad decisions, but I wasn't a bad person. "Would they tell you if they had a secret like that?" My life had taught me to never accept something at face value; most things were not what they seemed. People weren't always who they wanted you to believe. They had secrets and put on facades. "Think about it; does your family know everything about you? Is it so hard to believe they might have their private troubles too?"

He stiffened but shook his head. "Not like that. Not cheating. Not fathering another child."

My shoulders sagged. "Like I said, I ruled Kip out."

"I can't believe you took Noah's, Quinn's, and Bayden's hairs too? Do you have any idea how wrong that is? You invaded our privacy. You stole from us."

I felt like mold on bread and knew Ethan would toss me away.

"Why didn't you tell me all of this before?" His accusatory stare dug at my nerves, but I wasn't about to crumble in front of him. I'd wait until I was alone to fall apart.

"I didn't tell anyone. Do you know how awful it is to grow up not knowing who your father is? A kid should have access to information like health records and family history. Knowing where you came from helps mold you into the person you are. I came from nothing. I am nothing." I lifted a shoulder before letting it drop, my gaze drifting away from him toward my clean kitchen and to the door window that showed off the deep snow outside and the lazily drifting flakes still falling. "I mean, would you advertise something like that? My father could've been a criminal. I didn't want to say anything until I knew for sure." That was only a half-truth. I wasn't ready to tell Ethan my other secret. It was a moot point now. As soon as the snow cleared, he'd be gone.

"I don't give a damn what people think, so yeah, I would've spread that around like the wind." His eyebrows lowered and pushed toward one another as he furrowed his brow.

"You give a damn, Ethan. Come on, you told me that being picked last bothered you." I sat forward, fully invested in calling him out on his bullshit. "Imagine that, instead of being picked last, someone downright refused to let you be on their team. *That's* what my dad did. He didn't pick me at all. Imagine how that feels? I wasn't going to alert the media for a headline that read, Bastard Child Seeks Biological Father for Missed Holidays, Family History, and Hugs. A person should have access to all of that." A tear slipped from my eye, but I swiped it away.

"No." His features softened. "But maybe he didn't know."

Leave it to soft-hearted Ethan to have that idea. How does someone father a child and not know? Still, the implications and possibilities leave my thoughts reeling. My mom was a liar, so why did I believe her when she said he had died? Ethan could be right and my father didn't know. That certainly made him less of a monster, but not more of a father.

The possibility also cautioned me to be nice when I pointed fingers and explained myself to the man most likely to be my dad.

"Maybe you're right." I gave a half-hearted smile, but achiness trickled into the space around my heart and squeezed.

Agitation still danced in his eyes. "If you'd told me the truth in the beginning, I could've helped you come to that conclusion a long time ago." He glanced toward the window like he'd rather be anywhere but here. "If you'd trusted me instead of—"

"This wasn't about trust." He had my motives all wrong. "This was about me and finding out who I am, and where I come from." *And why I have this disease.* I shoved my plate away and scrubbed a spot on the coffee mug with my finger. "And while I don't know anything, I'm scared that speaking up and admitting I'm looking for someone will only make people more closed-lipped." I wished he'd meet my eyes, but he continued to stare outside as if that's where all the answers were.

It felt like a lifetime passed. Not being able to stand the silence, I said, "Please don't tell anyone." Now that my story existed outside my thoughts, I couldn't help but fear he'd talk and people would shun me. If he told everyone, I could kiss finding my birth father goodbye. I knew my mother, and I couldn't blame him for running from her, no matter his motivation. I would've run too if I was smarter and had the chance.

He didn't answer, and despite the rising warmth of the room, a chill settled beneath my skin. "Ethan, please don't say anything."

"Why did you befriend my family? Why did you chase after me so hard?" His eyes swept back to me. "I mean, you worked hard to get me to notice you and make me jealous. *Why?*"

My pulse kicked up, and nausea that had once eased came

back in full force. Beads of sweat prickled my forehead, and my entire body quaked.

He shook his head as if silently warning me not to lie. I struggled to think of how to tell him the truth without sounding awful.

"I like you, Ethan. I always have." That part wasn't a fabrication; I liked Ethan from the moment I laid eyes on him. My heart told me he was a good man, and I went with that instinct.

"But..." he hesitated, as though he knew the story didn't end with my liking him. He studied my face as the trembling radiated through me.

"Are you okay?" he asked, "You're pale suddenly."

The pain in my stomach increased, and I swallowed hard. That was a harder question to answer, so I went back to the first question. "Honestly, I thought the Lockhart family would know all the town secrets." As I spoke, I silently begged him to forgive me. "Your family is respected and has deep roots here. When you were just names on a piece of paper, it made sense to get to know you and see if you knew the truth. Now that I know you as people, I'm sorry for not telling you." The words pouring out of me were a relief.

My pulse pounded in my ears like roaring waves crashing on the beach, and the world flashed white around the edges. "I just hope you know that not telling you was my way of protecting myself and not my intention to hurt you."

CHAPTER TWELVE

ETHAN

HER WORDS RANG in my ears. *I just hope you know that not telling you was just my way of protecting myself and not my intention to hurt you.*

Was she protecting herself from me? From my family? What made her so vulnerable that she'd think she needed protecting?

She thought my family would have answers for her, so she pretended to be a friend and manipulated the situation to benefit her. She slithered her way into our lives with ulterior motives and plucked pieces of us for her benefit. I glanced at her again. Her ashen face, dotted with beads of sweat, worried me. "Are you okay?" I asked again, aware that she wasn't okay at all but unsure how to ask more directly without giving away that I'd gone through her medicine cabinet. I wasn't ready to admit that I too had done some snooping because mine was accidental, hers was intentional.

I regretted invading her privacy, but I couldn't go back and undo looking through her things. Did that make us even?

She rose on shaky legs, held up one finger in my direction in a clear *give me one minute* gesture, and made her way to the bathroom on limbs that didn't seem able to hold her upright. I was torn between being furious and worried about her health. My instinct sided with worry. We'd just been intimate, and I felt something for this woman. Something I shouldn't after knowing what she did to me and my family. I was torn on what to do, so I stood and paced the kitchen. Should I follow her or give her space?

The deception filled my mind. Plenty of people didn't know who their father was. Hell, plenty of people tracked their fathers down. How many of them hid what they were doing? To my knowledge, this wasn't a common method of handling the situation. She downright tricked me and my family.

I continued to pace, my thoughts spiraling out of control. Her affection and friendship started because she thought she could get information. She took DNA samples and manipulated everything. Could I forgive that? And now she tells me she's always had feelings for me? I didn't know what was real or fake anymore.

The ugly thoughts circled around and around in my brain.

I stared down the hallway toward the bathroom. She'd been gone a long time. "Everything okay?" I called out.

"Yeah." Her breathless response told me she was lying—again. "I need a quick shower."

Concerned, I walked to the door and pushed it open right as she flushed the toilet. The unmistakable sour smell of vomit filled the room, and I caught her wiping the back of her hand across her mouth. "I'll be fine." The full-body trembling hadn't eased, and worry filled my thoughts.

"Let me help you." With gentle hands, I supported her with one arm and pulled her shirt off with the other. She leaned into me as if seeking my body heat, and I helped her out of her shorts. I continued to be her balance as I scooted forward and turned on the water.

"Thank you," she whispered.

There were many questions I needed answered, but did I have a right to ask them when she was obviously ill? "You're welcome." I wound an arm around her ribs and helped her into the tub. "Why don't you sit?" I lowered her, and she folded neatly to the bottom. I grabbed the detachable showerhead, bringing it down to her level, sat on the edge, and ran the hot water over her back.

With her head down, she reminded me of a beautiful, broken statue of a fallen angel. Steam billowed through the room and fogged up the mirror, giving the space an ethereal look.

"Do you hate me?" Her quiet voice almost slipped past me.

"Why would I hate you?" I didn't hate her, but anger filled me as I thought about her lies and deception. Maybe anger was the wrong word because it sure felt like sadness and loss.

"For lying to you. For tricking you. For taking what wasn't mine." Her shoulders slumped as if the weight of the situation had shattered her. "I swear I didn't think there was another way."

"Did you take hair from everyone on that list?"

She shook her head. "No. After I did it to your family, it felt wrong. It was wrong, and I'm sorry. If I could go back in time, I'd do lots of things differently. I'd do anything to make sure you didn't hate me." Her voice cracked.

I was certain she was crying and couldn't handle that right now. "I don't hate you. I'm mad, but I don't hate you." She inhaled a shuddering breath as I moved the water across her shoulders. Her hair waved under the stream and plastered to her head while lengthening down her back. "Are you sick?" That seemed an innocent enough question; after all, I caught her on the heels of having thrown up.

"Yeah, but I'll be okay." She brought her legs to her chest and wound her arms around them before resting her forehead on her knees. The closed-off position said she wouldn't talk about whatever illness she faced.

Warmth crept across my skin, prickling hot, and I considered taking my shirt off. The hot water, the steam, the humidity overpowered me, but I focused on her well-being, not my discomfort.

"Anxiety?" I asked, totally out of my depth, but remembering another friend who suffered from debilitating anxiety. They'd also gotten sick during confrontational conversations and often threw up. I wasn't a doctor, and I didn't know what her medications were, so how could I know what she suffered from?

"No, not anxiety." She answered but didn't offer additional information to help me understand.

I continued to move the water around her shoulders, her back, and down her neck as she stayed in a protective, fetal position. The heat turned her skin rosy, and I contemplated turning it down, but she still shivered.

"What do we do now?" she asked.

I wasn't sure what she meant. "Well, I'll stay here and hold the water for you until you're ready to get out." Sweat beaded across my brow, and I wiped it away with the back of my hand. My shirt clung to my damp skin.

"I meant with *us*." Her miserable voice cracked with the last word, and I understood.

Us. I hadn't considered the future. Instead, I focused on taking care of her in the moment rather than thinking about what her revelations meant for tomorrow. "I'm not sure." Staying with someone I didn't trust wasn't an option. Given that she lied to me and deceived me while pretending to be my friend in an attempt to get something ... I didn't know if I could salvage anything between us.

She continued to tremble despite the hot water, and we fell into silence. Perched on the edge of the tub, I studied her slim frame and wished things were different. Running back through our friendship, I realized she'd lost weight since I first met her—a noticeable amount, too. Did I have any right to mention that? My mother taught me to only discuss a woman's weight or age at my own peril.

Had she eaten and thrown up? Perhaps it was an eating disorder? I shook my head. That made no sense because we'd eaten together, and she hadn't been sick afterward.

"What are you thinking about?" The skin between her ribs filled out then dipped slightly with her words.

"You. I'm worried about you."

She rubbed her hand over her face. "Don't worry about me. I'm a stubborn woman, but you know that." Her attempt to lighten the mood didn't succeed, and I exhaled. "You don't have to stay here with me, you know." As she spoke, she lifted her head and showed me her red cheeks and watery eyes. She reached for the showerhead, refusing to meet my gaze.

I pulled it back. "I don't mind." Of the many things I claimed to be, an asshole wasn't one of them. Even though I was upset with her, I wouldn't run out when she needed me. Right now, I'd hold the water for her until she finished and help her out of the tub and into clothes. I'd be by her side. After that ... I wasn't sure.

"I don't like that expression." She studied my face and tried to smile. "And I'm not saying I don't like your face. I do."

Again, her attempt to lighten the mood failed.

I couldn't stop thinking about whether she truly gave a damn about me. I would've told her everything I knew. My mother would've had a conversation with her. I couldn't think of a single person in town who wouldn't have shared the information she wanted if she had asked.

Instead, she lied and kept people she claimed to care about in the dark. Instead of trusting me, she used me. That fact hurt more than always being picked last.

What had she said about not being picked at all? Did she understand it was worse to be chosen under false pretenses and lied to by someone who not only claimed to care about me but someone I liked?

"I'm sorry," she whispered as if reading my mind.

I continued to move the water along her skin, wishing we could go back and do things differently.

"Before I came here and met you guys, I couldn't be sure you were good people. My mother was a broken woman, and she fractured things in me that I don't always know are fragmented." Her voice cracked, and I ached for her. As bad as I felt for her, it still didn't make what she'd done forgivable. You don't get to be a bad person and blame other people for your undesirable traits.

She knew lying was wrong, and I refused to believe she thought tricking people was acceptable.

"Did you figure out who your father is?" How soon would she be leaving town? I braced myself for the inevitable; once she got what she wanted, she'd no doubt leave.

"Not yet, but I think it's Roy."

That must have been the real reason she took the job at his bar. She planned to use him too; no doubt she'd wait for him to slip up, and then she'd spring it on him. "I hope you find out who your dad is. I don't think it'll fill whatever void you're hoping to fill, though."

She tightened her arms around her legs, the motion flexing the muscles under her soft, wet skin. "I just want to know who I am, and where I came from. You wouldn't understand because you know exactly who you are."

"You already have those answers." She knew her mother; she knew the person she'd become, and knowing her father wouldn't change any of that, would it?

"I don't think you understand what I mean." She curled up tighter somehow, and I wanted to lean in and wrap my arms around her. Instead, I kept my distance and warmed her skin by moving the water wand along her flesh.

What was the old adage? Fool me once, shame on you, fool me twice, shame on me. Letting her in and allowing her to use me again wasn't an option I'd consider.

"You're too quiet." Her soft voice left a hollow pain in my chest.

Things would get much quieter between us. There was no going back to what we had before. Maybe she deserved grace; after all, she was looking for her long-lost father, and her mother didn't seem like a nice person, but none of that gave her the right to do what she'd done.

CHAPTER THIRTEEN

ANGIE

WE SLEPT SEPARATELY LAST NIGHT, and I woke up several times running my hand between the sheets, searching for him. I sat up in bed, squinting into the sunlight, unsure what time of day it was, as the light glinted off the snow so brightly it blinded me through the opening in the curtains. Pulling my legs to my chest, I scanned the room while the previous night rose in my thoughts.

After he helped me out of the shower and allowed me to lean on him while I dressed, he was reticent. He'd been warm, kind, and understanding during the shower, and it meant everything having him there to support me while sickness overcame me. I was grateful for him, and those moments taught me I wanted him by my side always.

Every time I fell—be it off ladders or out of health like yesterday morning—Ethan was right where I needed him the most.

That hurt like hell because I had a feeling things between us were over before they'd gotten started. My chest ached with every heartbeat. While I kept my secrets to protect myself, hindsight told me I could've found a better way.

Honesty should've been paramount, but I messed up—badly. Throwing the blankets off, I stood and dressed, well aware that today was Tuesday. I should've been going to Silver Springs, but there was no way I could do that with the snow piled high outside.

I picked up my phone and stepped into my bathroom to take my morning medications while dialing the renal center. Waiting for them to answer, I swallowed the pills and stared at myself in the mirror. The dark circles under my eyes made me look like I hadn't slept in this lifetime. My cheeks seemed sunken in, and my lips were chapping to the point of flaking. How long had I been ignoring that thirsty sensation?

"Silver Springs Renal Center, can I help you?"

They wouldn't like this news, but there was nothing I could do to help it. "Hey, this is Angie. I wanted to let you know that I'm going to miss my treatment this week." My pulse thundered, causing my ears to ring.

The receptionist let out a noise that was a cross between a *hmm* and a grunt. "Missing dialysis isn't recommended."

I nodded as if she could see me, even though I knew she couldn't. "We're snowed in, and there's not much I can do unless I call for a Lifeline chopper." My weak attempt at humor was missed.

"Call them if you experience any of the symptoms your doctor has discussed with you. Keep taking your medication and take extra care of yourself. Oh, and stay warm, okay?" Her almost motherly concern brought a smile to my lips, and my anxiety about the conversation eased.

"I will, thank you." I thought about my thinning cheeks and chapped lips. Her nudge would be what it took for me to do better—that and missing this treatment. Treatments always made me feel tired but ultimately better.

"We'll see you on your next scheduled appointment." She said a quick goodbye, and I hung up the phone, staring at the screen as the time spent on the phone blinked at me. It was the first time I missed treatment since my diagnosis.

I tiptoed out of the bathroom and into my bedroom to stand by the window and stare at the snow. There was no way I could face Ethan. Not with all the stress pressing down on my shoulders with the weight of a dying star. I placed my hand against my back, just below the ribs, and ran it down. The heat in my flanks and the tenderness there made me wince.

Outside, the sun melted the snow, and I wondered if they'd plow my street.

If they did, Ethan would leave. That thought made my stomach ache. Running my tongue over my ragged lips, I sighed—I would have to face him, if only for the opportunity to get a glass of water. Steeling myself, I left my room and lumbered across the cool hardwood floor to the kitchen.

I filled a glass of water from the tap, thanking my lucky stars the pipes weren't frozen. My throat balked as I tipped it back and gulped the liquid.

The pain from my lower back and stomach often made eating and drinking difficult; that was one downside of growing that many cysts on my kidneys. Not that there were any upsides. I considered that statement and knew it wasn't true. There was one upside; my dad likely suffered the same genetic condition. Heck, if I had access to people's medical records, I'd know who my father was in no time. Too bad medical records were off-limits.

"Good morning." Ethan's voice startled me, and the water went down the wrong pipe. I choked, trying to cough it out while he hurried to my side. "I'm sorry, are you okay?" He gently tapped on my upper back with a flat palm. The thumping sensation radiated to my lower back, bringing waves of pain.

White fuzzed at the edges of my vision as cotton filled my head. Jerking away from his touch, I offered him what I hoped resembled a smile. "Thank you. I'm better." I held back another cough, disguising it as clearing my throat instead.

He frowned as he watched me. "Are you sure you're okay?"

He kept asking me that question. I studied his handsome face, wondering if telling him the truth would be a better idea. After all, lying to him had damn near destroyed things between us. But lying about looking for my dad wasn't the same as not telling him about my health.

"I'm not feeling well." There. That was honest. What was the point in telling him when he was walking out of my life any minute?

"I'm sorry to hear that. Can I help?" His serious expression reminded me why I hated telling people the truth—the pity I found in their eyes destroyed me.

I shook my head. "Thank you, but no."

His gaze ticked to the window. "I think the snow melted off enough for me to leave, unless you need me."

My heart screamed yes, I needed him, but my head knew better. I'd broken his trust, and he told me that was unforgivable. A relationship with Ethan was no longer an option.

"I'll be okay. Please drive safely." I wouldn't beg him to stay if he already decided to go.

He gave a terse nod, then headed for the front door.

"Talk to you later?" I asked with hope in my voice.

He nodded, pulled the door open to a wave of cold air, and walked out.

I finished my water and placed the glass on the counter, silently reminding myself to drink more soon. With soft steps, I crept to the door and peeked out the glass. Ethan walked back from his truck with a shovel in hand and cleared my walkway of snow. I watched him work and nodded at Max as the mailman brought my mail to the door.

I opened it and took the mail, ushering Max inside with a wince, as pain exploded through my lower back.

His head cocked to the side, and concern painted his expression.

"I'm okay," I gasped as he tried to steady me.

"Really, because you look like you're in pain."

Lifting both shoulders as if that gesture would add a layer of believability to my statement, I said, "I'm fine."

"Sure, you are," he mumbled under his breath.

"Do you want coffee or tea?" I tried to blink back the tears that threatened to spill. I'd been offering him coffee or tea all winter, and I wouldn't stop because of a little back pain.

He hesitated, then gave me a quick hug and guided me to the couch. Lowering down onto it, I smiled up at him as he spread the throw I kept hung over the back across my legs.

"You relax and take care of yourself. I'll see you tomorrow." With a smile and a wink, he left my place as I heard the rumble of Ethan's truck fade away.

A knock on the door dragged me out of a dream about Ethan; his scent still clung to the couch where I'd fallen asleep. I bolted upright, hoping he'd been the one to knock, and hurried to the door as best I could and opened it to find Roy and Gypsy.

"Max told you I was sick, didn't he?" I asked, suspicious as I noticed the brown paper bag in Roy's hands.

Gypsy nodded and pulled me into a gentle hug. "We brought you soup. I hope you get to feeling better."

"And don't hesitate to call if you need anything, kiddo." Roy's kind smile warmed my heart.

"Thank you." I accepted the brown paper bag and felt the warmth through the bottom. "I'll call if I need anything. I appreciate this, you guys." As far as family went, I could count on Roy and Gypsy. If Roy was my dad, I would consider myself lucky.

"Do you want to come in?" I asked.

Gypsy shook her head as Roy answered. "Gotta get back to the bar, but another time, all right?"

"Oh," Gypsy said as if remembering something important. "I wanted to thank you for those resources for Isla's project. It's coming along beautifully."

I gave a slight bow, instantly wishing I hadn't, because pain screamed up my back. "You're very welcome," I ground out the words. "I'm glad to have helped."

"Project?" Roy glanced at Gypsy.

She nodded, staring up at him. "I told you about it; the one she's doing about her family history."

My heart pounded in my chest. This moment might be the one where I found myself caught, and I wasn't ready for it.

"Oh." Roy smiled. "I remember now that Angie helped you with that."

Gypsy nodded but said nothing more. Instead, she pressed her lips together and raised her eyebrows as if she were giving me a silent promise to keep my secret. That gesture left me wondering if she'd figured me out. If she had, I appreciated her holding her tongue.

They turned to leave, but not before Gypsy gave me a little wave, and Roy flashed a warm smile. I grinned through the pain as they headed to his truck together. Carrying the sack into the kitchen, I set it on the stove and tore the stapled flaps apart. Inside, a Styrofoam cup held soup, and a tinfoil wrapped garlic bread bowl rested beside it. They brought an electrolyte-packed drink that I quickly took out and sipped as I served myself their thoughtful dinner.

They were good people, no doubt about that.

As far as father figures went, Roy proved daily that he'd be a fantastic dad, and with Gypsy by his side, the two were a power duo of love, support, and kindness.

Sadness cut through my joy as I wished Ethan had stayed, if only to share this meal with me.

CHAPTER FOURTEEN

ETHAN

WEDNESDAY MORNING BROUGHT MORE SNOWMELT, but I was too busy pacing my living room to notice. Everything with Angie kept me up at night and messed with my head significantly. I'd been so sure she liked me. Now I couldn't help but wonder if she only pretended to like me to get close enough to get information.

She didn't know her father. I ached for her situation because my father had meant so much to me. He'd been my rock, my model of the type of man I wanted to be, and he taught me the most valuable lessons I'd learned to date.

Not a single day went by that I didn't have at least a passing thought of him. I couldn't imagine growing up without him. Even though I understood that Angie's position must be difficult, that didn't excuse her actions.

My phone chimed, and I stopped pacing to pull it out of my pocket. The text from Angie lit my screen, and I opened the full message. *Thank you for helping me get to work. You don't have to anymore.*

My chest compressed, burning like someone had punched me in the sternum. Being shut out of her life hurt, but not as much as her betrayal. I tapped the text box to respond. *You're welcome, but* I didn't hit send. I stood there, staring at the message, wondering if there was any point in sending it. *I don't know how to fix this. I want to, but I don't know how.* I still didn't send the message. Instead, I held down the back arrow until the blinking cursor deleted every single letter. Touching the power button, I shut off the screen and shoved the phone back into my pocket.

Talking to her wouldn't change what she'd done. Movement outside caught my eye, and I glanced up in time to see Max walking to my mailbox. He opened the flap, shoved the mail inside, then peeked at the house, no doubt surprised I wasn't at the door to say hello and invite him in.

Without hesitation, I opened it and waved. A smile crossed his lips, and he waved back. Gesturing him toward me, I waited for him to walk up. The snow might melt, but the chill promised winter wasn't over yet.

Max stopped in front of me, and I noticed the white at his temples seemed to spread. "Tea, cocoa, or coffee today?"

"Water, if you don't mind." Max's voice brought a smile to my lips.

"There must be a bug going around." I could only imagine Max asking for water if he had an upset stomach. It was simply out of character for him. Given that Angie also seemed to have come down with something, that line of thinking made sense.

"Oh, I'm not sick. I just need to drink more water." Max studied me for a moment. "You look like something is on your mind today. Does it have anything to do with you being at Angie's house yesterday?"

He certainly was perceptive. I pulled a glass out of the cabinet and filled it under the tap before offering it to him. He took it with a smile and waited in silence, no doubt for me to start talking.

With a heavy sigh, I began. "She used me. In fact, she's using everyone."

Max nearly spit out his water before giving me a disapproving glance. "You have something to back up that accusation, right?" He sounded almost disappointed, but I knew he'd change his tune when I told him everything.

I sat down at the kitchen table, and he leaned against the counter, still taking sips of his water. "She told me she knew we were a well-respected family in town, that others trusted us, and that we'd likely have the information she needed."

"Information she needed? For what?" He studied me thoughtfully, without a hint of the anger I expected.

Did the reason matter? There was no excuse for what she'd done.

"She's looking for her dad. Instead of just asking, she's been sneaking around and manipulating people to get what she wants." Even now, the thought made my skin prickle. I'd fallen for her tricks, and I had no one to blame but myself.

Max stayed silent for a moment, shifted his weight, and finished his water. I watched him refill the glass and take another sip as he considered what I said. Pulling my phone out of my pocket, I placed the device on the table. Planting my elbows on the wooden surface, I waited for his response.

I wasn't sure what there was to think about. Max could never come up with a reason to justify her actions.

"I've spent a long time in this town," Max said slowly, his gaze focused on some point far in the distance. "One thing I've learned is that nobody gives up their secrets willingly."

Did he believe that?

"Max, if she came to you right now and asked if you're her dad, would you tell her the truth?" We could simplify this argument right now by making it personal.

"Well, of course, I would now, because I know her." Max snorted while holding the glass in his palm and rotating it in a slow circle. "But in the beginning, when she first got to town, I might have assumed she was some new scammer, or that she asked for the wrong reasons."

I hadn't thought of that.

"She had to get to know people first. Nobody is going to tell their secrets to a stranger." Max turned and placed his cup in the sink. His hand hovered near the dishcloth for a moment, but I quickly stopped him.

"Don't you dare." He knew better than to wash dishes in my home.

He turned back around, a smile beaming from his face. "She got to know us, but she did so under false pretenses because what other choice did she have?"

He made far too much sense. Uncomfortable, I shifted in my seat. Had I been wrong about everything? Maybe I'd been unfair to her because Max had a valid point. No one shared their secrets with a stranger. Hadn't she said something similar? Why did it sound more reasonable coming from Max? *Because you're not in love with Max.* That thought made me reel. I had strong feelings for Angie, but love?

"Think about it." Max put an elbow on the counter, angling

his body toward me in a way that said I had one hundred percent of his attention. "If she told people she was here looking for her dad from the start, they would likely assume the worst or not trust her, especially in today's world where we face constant scams. She wasn't safe to tell anyone, and instead, she came here, got to know everyone, kept a secret, and tried to get the information she needed to *find her father.*" He emphasized the words *her father.* "Kip meant the world to you. Imagine not having him. Imagine a void inside you that nothing fills. Imagine not knowing where you come from. Wouldn't you do anything to get those answers?" His intensity grew, though his posture stayed nonthreatening.

He'd taken my make-it-personal tactic and turned it back on me. *Well played, Max, well played.* I didn't appreciate his efforts because he was right. Facing the situation presented, I would do anything to find my father. Even if it meant not being completely honest with everyone around me.

That didn't make what she'd done less painful.

"It's hard to see because it's personal for you. You feel betrayed and attacked." Max seemed to read my mind again. "But would you have done the same in her place?"

I would have, but I wasn't ready to admit that yet.

"Also, people might protect one another. I know I wouldn't give up any of your secrets, or anyone else's, for that matter. And I doubt you'd give up anyone's either." He lifted a shoulder, and I knew he was right. I wouldn't talk about someone else's business. The only reason I was talking about her now was I needed advice, and I trusted Max.

"Remind me to never debate you, Max." His reasoned logic and ability to step outside the situation left me feeling like I was wrestling outside my weight class—I couldn't win. Not that I was trying to win. I glanced down at the table, at my phone, feeling guilty for not responding to her, for giving her grief, for not being a better friend. She deserved more, but I'd been so blinded by my feelings that I'd messed it all up. While I still felt betrayed by her, I understood why she'd done it.

He chuckled. "Also, I want you to ask yourself who in this town would willingly give up their secrets. I know it stunned you and your brothers to find out I was married."

I jerked my head up to stare at him. He was a prime example of someone that didn't share, but I had no doubt that he knew everyone's business in town. "Do you know who her father is?"

He shook his head. "I don't, but I'll certainly put out feelers now that I know she's looking."

"Oh, you're not going to tell anyone, are you?" Fear swept through me. "I shouldn't have told you."

Max held a finger to his lips. "I'm the master of keeping secrets, and I'll keep this one."

I sighed with relief. "Thank you. And thank you for helping her."

He moved toward the door, and I stood up to follow. As he turned, I noticed a glint in his eyes. "This town has a lot of secrets, Ethan."

I nodded. I knew that with certainty.

The thought reminded me of another one ... the one she kept in her medicine cabinet. "Oh, she also takes a lot of medications, and I noticed she's also losing weight."

Max held up a finger. "If you're about to ask me if she's abusing prescriptions, I'll have you know I won't engage in that kind of speculation. Unless you saw other people's names on the bottles—which you shouldn't have checked—I don't want to have this discussion."

I worried about her, but I also considered the potential for something darker. "Not suggesting abuse, just that she seems young to take so many medications."

"You are suggesting abuse, then." Max sighed. "I take daily medications too. Medications prescribed by my doctor. You have to realize that some people fight battles you know nothing about. Most people will not share their medical issues with you, even if they trust you or know you. She doesn't owe you answers."

I sighed. "You keep making too much sense, Max."

He nodded. "Somebody has to remind you that other people are just that—imperfect humans." His gaze met mine. "Like you."

I winced. "Thanks for the reminder." I wasn't sarcastic at all. I had no right to judge anyone because I had flaws.

"Stop looking for things to be upset over. If you think you could love her, support her. If you don't think you can love her, make sure she knows, so she can move on." Max stepped outside, and I followed.

For the first time, I felt like I disappointed him, and it felt the same as when I disappointed my father.

I also worried he had a good reason to be unhappy with me. I'd known Angie since she arrived in Cross Creek. She was good people, and because my heart was involved, and it was, I allowed doubt to creep inside. Doubt was love's poison.

CHAPTER FIFTEEN

ANGIE

I DIDN'T NEED Ethan to continue my search, but his support would've been nice.

Straightening my coat with a sharp tug of the material, I stared at the front of the bar for a moment. The marching line of windows offered warmth in the biting cold. The decorations and lights Ethan and I had hung added to the welcoming charm of the place. My mouth dried out like I'd left it open in the heat of a desert, and my pulse drummed in my ears. Today everything would change.

Inside, I saw Roy in his usual spot behind the bar and glimpsed Gypsy sitting in a booth. Other than the two of them, the bar stood empty. It wasn't my day to work, but I didn't see Kandra either. They must have decided not to call me because I'd been so sick.

That hurt because I worked very hard to keep my illness hidden from everyone. I didn't want anyone to feel bad for me or treat me differently because of my health. One lousy day had been all it took to blow my cover.

I stalled. My legs trembled, my hands shook, and my lungs burned with every breath of icy air. I didn't want to go inside or have the conversation that needed to happen. However, it was the time to be strong, and there was no use pretending I could keep putting this off.

With a shiver, I pulled open the door and walked inside. The heat hit me like a brick oven, and I thawed out as the scent of beer and garlic tickled my nose. My stomach growled, and I tried to remember the last time I'd eaten. Was it the day before? Roy's soup and garlic bread bowl? Had I eaten anything today?

I didn't think I had.

"Hi, Angie. Feeling better?" Roy's voice greeted my frozen ears, and Gypsy glanced up at me with a kind smile.

"A lot better." Despite my cheery tone, dread knotted my stomach as I thought about the conversation I'd be springing on them soon. I didn't envy the shock they were going to endure, but I couldn't think of another way to do things.

When I came to Cross Creek, I thought the talk would be the simple part—I'd been wrong. Nothing about the adventure had been simple. Every step of the way was a nightmare. Even falling for Ethan had ended in disaster.

"Thanks for bringing me food yesterday." What if they hated me after I accused Roy of being my father? What if Roy admitted he actually had knocked up my mom without knowing and then resented me for existing? I mean, my research had shown that people didn't like facing surprises and proof of mistakes they made. And anyone that had been with my mom probably considered their encounter a blunder. There was no way around that.

What if this conversation destroyed the friendship I'd built with Roy and Gypsy like the truth had wrecked mine and Ethan's relationship?

"Uh-oh." Gypsy furrowed her brow at me, and I knew she caught on to the serious nature of my visit. Her voice seemed to draw Roy's attention, and he came around the bar with a worried look on his face.

"Is everything okay?" he asked.

I nodded, then reconsidered, and shook my head.

He put an arm around my shoulders without quite weighing me down and ushered me toward Gypsy. I followed his guidance, crossing my fingers that this whole conversation would be smooth and straightforward with no anger or hard feelings. While I wished he'd welcome me with open arms, I prepared for the worst.

We stopped at the booth, and he took the spot beside Gypsy while I sat in the seat opposite them.

I took a deep breath, reminding myself why the conversation had to happen now. The close call yesterday woke me up to the possibility that I'd get caught keeping secrets, and Ethan's reaction to it warned me that not everyone would be happy or kind when they found out why I'd come to town. I pulled my phone out of my pocket and glanced down at the screen. He still hadn't responded to my text, and that left a hollow ache low in my belly.

"What's on your mind?" Gypsy asked.

I inhaled a deep breath, held it for a moment, then released it a molecule at a time. Struggling to gather every last crumb of courage I possessed, I stared at the wooden table that had been waxed and buffed to an incredible, warm shine. My heart picked up its pace, and dizziness overcame me.

"I think you're my dad." I glanced at Roy and watched his

mouth open slightly in stunned silence as his eyes went wide. Gypsy inhaled sharply and put her hand over his on the table. Her other hand found mine, and her warm touch offered comfort to my freezing fingers. "I found records that you were here right around the time my mom got pregnant. You were the right age, the right type for my mom…" I rattled off the evidence I'd gathered, but as I spoke, I could hear how weak my conclusions were.

Gypsy glanced from me to Roy, her gaze filled with sorrow as he slowly shook his head.

I trailed off, wondering why he was gesturing no. My pulse continued to race, and that faint sensation had me gripping the table for support and internally swearing not to pass out.

"No, what?" I asked, needing him to speak up and say something, *anything*. The silence rang so loudly in my ears, I worried I'd gone deaf.

"I can't be your dad, Angie." Roy's calm, kind voice brought tears to my eyes. He gently reached out and gathered my hands up with his own, his warm eyes locked on mine. I let him hold on to me, desperately needing comfort.

"How do you know that for sure?" I whispered. "Everybody makes mistakes. I wouldn't think less of you. My mom never told anyone anything about herself. Not the truth, anyway."

Gypsy let out a soft sound of anguish and grabbed my forearm with one hand, giving it a reassuring squeeze. I could see the pain shining in her eyes, and her warmth sank into my chilled skin.

Roy's certainty stopped me up short. His expression left no doubt that he knew for sure he wasn't my dad, and that thought poked at me. Tears overflowed my lower lids, and I pulled away from them to wipe away the dampness. Roy quickly offered me a clean towel, and I buried my face in the material for a second, hating how hard all of this was. This battle was mine alone, and I'd never met someone my age struggling through it, which left me feeling more isolated than I'd ever felt in my life.

"Angie, I had a vasectomy."

The blood in my veins stopped moving, though my heart thumped double time. I hadn't considered that possibility. Not that it mattered if I had; medical records are the Holy Grail of the unattainable. I lifted my head out of the towel and dropped the linen on the table. Staring at him, I shook my head, not believing for a second what he was saying. My heart betrayed me and whispered that Roy wouldn't lie about something like that.

"Back when I was eighteen, I knew I never wanted to have kids." He stopped when Gypsy nudged him with an elbow. He glanced at her, and then his attention bounced back to me as if he understood what she was trying to tell him. "I mean, you'd be the person I hope my kids would become if I did, but I can't have children."

How had I been so wrong? Where was the mistake? And who could be my father?

No. I hadn't made a mistake. "Vasectomies can fail." Maybe he just didn't know. Roy might have been my dad, even if he didn't want to admit that possibility.

"Angie, it has an extremely low failure rate. The odds are so low—"

"Have you checked?" If he hadn't had a sperm count check, I wouldn't be sure that I wasn't his kid.

He shook his head. "Well, no, but..." He glanced at Gypsy as if silently begging for help.

"What if he took a paternity test?" She glanced at me with her kind eyes filled with sorrow.

"I'll do that. I'll take a test as soon as I can, and we'll settle this." Roy seemed relieved with her idea, and my stomach knotted tighter. He was so sure he wasn't my dad that it shook my belief in his ability to be my father. A vasectomy. Why hadn't I considered that? And Roy hadn't wanted kids?

I remembered the ace up my sleeve. "I can prove it," I said, standing up as if my ah-ha moment propelled me upright. They both stared at me in stunned surprise, and I lowered back into my seat. Excitement left a tremble in my voice, and I tried to keep my tone low and calm as I spoke.

"Family medical history ... you have polycystic kidney disease." I stared at him, waiting for the response. "It's a genetic disease."

He glanced at Gypsy, who lifted her shoulders a fraction of an inch, then his attention came back to me.

"I don't know what that is, hon."

My heart sank. "Surely someone in your family has polycystic kidney disease?" As if saying the name made mine flair, pain cut through my lower back and up into my abdomen. With a grimace, I tried to ignore it as I waited for Roy to tell me of some aunt or someone who had mentioned the disease.

He shook his head. "The only thing that runs in my family is my nephew Doug. He's a marathon runner." Despite his attempt at humor, I couldn't muster a smile. The reality that he might be right finally sank in. The realization that this entire trip, and all the research I'd done, amounted to nothing was like a powerful kick in the gut.

I sat across from them, shell-shocked and speechless. Breathless. Empty-headed. Frozen. The universe seemed to have stood still, and I found myself stuck in that moment.

Roy wasn't my father.

"We're still family, no matter what the paternity test says," Gypsy said, pushing Roy out of the booth to come and wind her slim, sinewy arms around me. Roy stood over us for a second before retaking his spot.

My heart seemed to have stopped beating, and blood felt stagnant in my veins. As tears burned my eyes, I wished Ethan was beside me with his arms around me to hold me tightly. I needed his words of comfort, his kindness, his promises that everything would be okay. I needed his support—support that had run out, all because I hadn't been totally honest.

CHAPTER SIXTEEN

ETHAN

"YOU LET it go a little longer than usual." Patti's voice held a note of happiness I hadn't heard from her before. I smiled as she fired up the clippers and ran them up the back of my head. Spiky, itchy hair rained down on the black sheeting she'd whipped around my shoulders and slid to the floor as I sat in her barber chair facing the windows.

"I know." Usually, I was in here every two weeks getting trimmed up, and Patti was always a delight. She usually tried to play matchmaker, and I knew she'd been trying to maneuver Angie and me together. The clippers went quiet, and the scent of alcohol filled my nose as she swirled her comb in the disinfectant.

"Did you miss me?" Her teasing tone, as the comb slid through my hair and her scissors clipped and snipped here and there, left me feeling at home. I'd been in this chair almost every two weeks for the last ten years. I remembered when her mother ran the place, and she worked here. Her mother had since moved to Florida, tired of the wet and cold here, and now Patti ran the business.

"Of course, I did. How have you been?" After my fallout with Angie, the normalcy of having my hair cut was a welcomed distraction. The more I thought about Angie, the more upset I became. Dying for more work, I tried to talk my brothers into taking on some easy, short-term projects, but they all dragged their feet and offered poor excuses. My brothers knew how to drive me insane.

"Good." She lowered her voice as if imparting a secret. "I met someone."

"Oh?" I wasn't the type to gossip, but I didn't mind letting her tell me about her life. She'd been lonely after her mother left, and she'd always been such a kind person. With her little shop on the main street and being the only hair care shop around, she seemed to be the heartbeat of the town.

"Miranda got me into online dating, and I met a very nice man." She continued to fuss over my hair, her attention to detail typical. Her haircuts were always crisp, clean, and well worth the cost.

"You have to be careful with that," I warned, but she clicked her tongue at me.

"Miranda made sure I knew how to approach it safely. She offered all kinds of information. I owe her for all her help." She turned the clippers on for a moment and cleaned up the back of my neck. When the hum went quiet, she resumed talking as if there'd been no break. "He's sweet. His name is Albert, and we share so much in common, and the things we don't have in common, we are getting each other into." Pride filled her voice. "I went kayaking with him. I'd never been, but I had so much fun."

"That's wonderful." She deserved to be happy. And knowing Miranda helped her earned her points for kindness.

"Thank you. So how are you and Angie?" She ran the comb along the top of my head, trimming up as I watched the cars go by. She knew I preferred to watch outside while she cut my hair. That's why she faced me toward the windows.

That loaded question would've made me squirm if she hadn't been holding scissors a couple of inches from my head. "We're friends." I didn't want to get into that talk, nor would I give away anything I knew. Though she deceived me, I didn't have the right to tell her secrets.

Patti snorted. "Friends? You know you don't have to lie to me."

I grinned. "I'm not lying. We are friends."

"I see. Let's get this mess washed, shall we?" She whisked the protective plastic off my shoulders and guided me to the sinks. A moment later, she ran warm water over my scalp while rubbing some incredible-smelling shampoo into a lather on my head. "I think you two should try to be more than friends," she said casually as she gently scrubbed my head with her fingertips. "You'd be a cute couple, and friendships are the best place to start a romantic relationship."

"I'll take that into consideration." No way would I tell her the reason I wouldn't be considering her suggestion.

She rinsed my hair. "Want me to dry it?" she asked while gently towel-drying my head.

I shook my head. I didn't mind the shock of cold on my wet hair on the short walk to my truck.

She chuckled. "You're a madman."

"I know." I stood up and followed her to the front, running a hand through my damp hair as I moved. I paid and left her a handsome tip, offered a smile, a thanks, and exited, thinking about

Angie every step of the way. I let out a breath that turned to a silver cloud drifting toward the heavens.

My phone chimed, and I pulled it out of my pocket. A text popped up from Angie, and I unlocked the screen to read the entire message, my heart sinking.

Roy isn't my father. He's willing to get a paternity test, but I already know he's not. I thought you might want to know.

I did, and I didn't. My feelings about the situation were confusing; a mixed bag of anger, warmth, sadness, betrayal, worry, and love. I wished things were different.

Another text from her followed. *You're the only person who knows. I wish we could talk about it.*

That cry for help twisted my gut. I felt like a jerk for not being there when she texted she needed me, but I needed to protect myself too.

I needed more time to think through things, but for now, I had the sensation that I lost a limb. Angie and I had forged a friendship. I wasn't lying about that. It was a friendship and more. Love danced around the edges just waiting for a partner. But could I ever trust her again? I wasn't sure.

My truck beeped as I mistakenly hit the lock button on the fob instead of the unlock, and had to do it again. I opened the doors and climbed into the driver's seat, still staring at her texts. I couldn't respond right away; I needed time to figure out the right words.

The engine fired to life as I turned over the key and pulled out of the parking lot, nosing my truck toward home. As I drove, thoughts of her filled my mind, and the sticky situation offered no solutions. There didn't seem to be any good outcomes or straightforward answers.

I couldn't stop thinking about Max's disapproval of my reaction. When he found out, it upset me that he'd taken Angie's side. When I told him that Angie had been using everyone, he surprised me with his anger toward me.

He had several valid points, but I had a right to be upset about her actions, even if she'd been justified in making them.

Sure, the town held on to secrets. There was Kandra and her pregnancy. Miranda and her sister. My father and his heart problems. There were secrets all over the place, but did that excuse lying, manipulating, and tricking people? I didn't think so.

She had my father's name on her list. That felt so disrespectful to his memory, but despite that, I continued to hear his voice in my head telling me that in a world where you can be anything, always choose to be kind. I needed to do better.

I couldn't imagine not knowing my father. That would eat me up inside.

I pulled into my driveway and turned off my truck. Sitting behind the wheel for a few moments, I stared at my phone. Her messages on the screen called out to some part of me that wanted to respond. I cared about her, and it killed me to ignore her unmistakable cry for help.

I wish you'd have just been honest with me from the start, and I'm sorry your search hit another roadblock.

I didn't have to wait long. *I wish I had been, too. It's too late to change it, but please know I didn't tell anyone. I didn't trust anyone. As for the roadblock. I'm used to them. You'd understand if you knew my mother.*

Angie never talked about her mother, her past, or really about herself at all. I knew a few things, but getting personal information from her had always been a challenge, and the few things she shared were heartbreaking.

I climbed out of my truck and made my way to the front door. The chill of my home stung, and I wanted to turn up the heat, wishing the place didn't feel empty and cold. I made a beeline for the thermostat and cranked it up.

I want you in my life, no matter who my dad is.

Words were words. Her actions mattered...

How can I ever trust you again?

A moment ticked by, then another.

You'd have to take my word for it. You are my friend, Ethan. I'm sorry for what I did, and I wish I could change it all and start over.

Life has no do-overs. I wished for a do-over after my father died. Finding out he'd hidden his heart condition—the same condition that stole his life away—left me wishing I'd done more, that I'd been around more, that I'd called more... all those damn regrets wouldn't exist if he would've told me he was dying.

You didn't respect me enough to be honest with me. That's not friendship. I took a seat on the couch as warmth filled the room.

Her response came instantly. *Not at the start, no. You didn't trust me in the beginning either, did you?*

Well, no, but I also hadn't been hiding things from her, lying, and planning on using her, all things that were not a good foundation to build on.

Look, I think we have something special, Ethan. My feelings for you are honest and genuine.

I stared at the text. Were these words finally the truth? How would I know? That was the problem. Like Cindy, I couldn't trust her. I was right to keep my heart guarded.

CHAPTER SEVENTEEN

ANGIE

CURLED up on my couch watching TV with Ross in the background saying Rachel's name at his wedding rather than Emily's, I stared at my phone. A half-full container of double fudge brownie ice cream sat melting on my coffee table, and the scent of a lavender-vanilla candle I had lit filled the air.

Yep, I couldn't deny falling apart while I texted back and forth with Ethan. I'd pay for the dairy, which doesn't do well for my illness, but somehow, I was stuck between *screw it* and *worth it*. I hadn't been hungry the last few days, but no doubt that had something to do with the stress I'd been under. How many times could I tell Ethan I was sorry for what I'd done? How many times did he need to hear it before he accepted it as the truth?

I inhaled the comforting scent of the candle and reached for the carton of ice cream. Digging out a brownie bite and scraping up a ribbon of fudge, I shoved the spoon into my mouth and stared at my phone. He'd been taking a long time to message back for most of the conversation. I worried he was too busy moving on with his life and couldn't be bothered to talk to me.

I set the ice cream back down in the puddle of condensation. My junk food binge would come back to haunt me, but I found myself not giving a damn. Roy wasn't my dad. We sent out the paternity test, but I held zero hope it would come back positive.

Back to square one of the crappy game show that my life seemed to have turned into; *Who's My Daddy?* I'd been so sure it was Roy.

Did you do anything fun today? I texted.

Honestly, I craved some kind of meaningful connection. Preferably with Ethan, but sheesh, exhaustion and sadness were too much to bear.

No.

At least he responded. Even though I hated the one-word answers. I doubled down to coax something out of him. Anything would be better than monosyllabic responses.

I didn't leave the house. Did you at least enjoy some sunshine? Got a haircut.

Okay, progress. No complaints. Three words.

You were looking kind of scruffy.

No response. With a sigh, I turned the TV down as the episodes of *Friends* continued to play. Usually, the show made me smile, but nothing seemed to work these days.

I've been thinking about you all day.

I might as well put it all out there. I couldn't get him off my mind no matter how hard I tried. When had life gotten so impossibly hard?

I pulled my favorite blanket tight around my shoulders and tucked it in at my hip to stop the cooler air from sneaking in.

Can you forgive me?

Ugh, I sounded like a pathetic mess. He didn't want to talk to me, so why did I keep pushing? Because he meant the world to me, and I wanted things to go back to the way they were before he noticed the "hit list" on my bedside table. I wanted to wake back up in bed with him, grinning from ear to ear and unable to believe the lucky turn my life had taken.

I don't know, Angie.

That text stabbed through my heart like a blade covered in spikes, tearing out bits of flesh as it slid through.

The dots scrolled on the screen. He wasn't done.

I thought I could live with the flirting.

Flirting? Were we back to that again?

But everything else... I just don't know.

I'd been texting him, hoping to feel better. I thought he could help me shoulder some of this burden and help me through. Instead, his texts only added to my suffering.

I'm sorry, Ethan. I swear, if I could fix this, I'd go back in time and be honest from the get-go.

Maybe if I keep saying those words, he'd know I meant them, and it would help him change his mind. I felt him slipping away, and it was breaking my heart.

That's just it. You can't. There's no going back, and there are no do-overs. There's no fixing this. It's broken.

I inhaled as tears spilled over my lower lashes to slide down my cheeks. Something so final in his words broke me. If I didn't know better, I'd think he was telling me we had no chance of getting back together; whatever we had permanently ended in his mind.

What are you saying, exactly?

I needed to hear him say the words. Maybe I should call him, but my hands trembled so hard I couldn't dial before his message came in.

I'm saying that I'm done. Whatever you manufactured between us is over.

I stared at his text, my heart breaking into shards. My search turned out to be all for nothing. I never found my father. I'd lost Ethan. And my health seemed on a slippery downhill slope.

Stunned and shaking, I sat there, staring at his text, reading his words over and over as my eyes blurred, tears fell, and my vision fuzzed out again. We were through. He left no room for misinterpretation, no hope that we could repair things. No chance that maybe this would all blow over like the snowstorm we'd been caught in.

And his cruel choice of words ... what I *manufactured* between us. He didn't believe my feelings for him or his for me were genuine.

A knock at my door made me jolt in place, but I wasn't in the mood for company. I ignored whoever stood on my step, trying to hold back tears as I crept to the bathroom. The blood in my urine didn't startle me—common symptom—the pain didn't surprise me —also common—but the extreme nausea was new.

I stood, my shoulders hunched as my stomach twisted and bile pushed into my throat. Unable to hold back, despite swallowing like crazy, I inhaled. My skin prickled white-hot. The sudden heat bothered me, and I realized the tickling sensations down my back and sides were sweat.

Trembling deep in my core, I took another deep breath and let it slowly escape as whoever stood outside my door knocked again. Unable to stop myself, I gagged, heaving as my guts turned inside out.

Double fudge brownie ice cream was not friendly the second time around. The pain in my back intensified as I leaned forward, spitting out the sour saliva before another gag had me heaving. Only when I felt confident there was nothing left for me to puke did I stop, rinse out my mouth, and brush my teeth. Try as I might, I couldn't get rid of the metallic taste of blood.

Running my tongue over every inch of my mouth, I searched for some injury that might bleed but didn't find a tender spot or a hint of damage. Maybe I imagined things.

A hiccup caught me unaware, and I internally asked what else could go wrong. Hiccups might not bother most people, but my back and belly, already tender from my illness, found them excruciatingly painful.

Exhausted from throwing up, I turned on the shower, desperate to rinse the sweat from my still-prickling skin. As I pulled my clothing off, I ran my nails up and down every inch of my body, hoping to rid myself of the itchy, sticky feeling. Catching sight of myself in the mirror, I noticed the way my sharp shoulders poked up and realized I could count every rib. I knew I lost weight, an unfortunate side effect, but this seemed worse than I initially thought.

I crawled into the shower, resting my head on the edge, and let the hot water run over me.

I woke, curled up in the tub, the water cold on my freezing skin. Shivering violently, I could hardly sit up and turn it off. I tried to rub some feeling back into my numb legs with my tingling hands.

Unable to do so, I struggled my way out of the shower, pulled a towel around my shoulders, then yanked another one from the linen shelf. Covering myself in them, I curled up by the baseboard heater and let the warm air seep into my icy body as the urge to throw up filled me again.

Too weak to move, I laid there in a fetal position, as my stomach twisted and turned. The only thing stopping me from throwing up had to be that nothing was left in my system. Thank goodness for small favors.

I recognized the symptoms, and it scared the hell out of me.

Laying there, I stared at the wall, watching white fuzzies dance across the paint as pain filtered through me. Nothing was right, and I knew I was in trouble.

Where had I left my phone? A sharp ringing in my ears drowned out my thoughts as the blurring figures continued to dance back and forth on the wall. I gave into them and closed my eyes.

Jerking awake, I tossed the towels aside and sat up. Pain echoed through my body, and thirst plagued me. The darkness outside told me I'd been out for hours. That metallic taste in my mouth hadn't gone away but had intensified, and I crawled to the shower faucet, turned it on cold, and gulped the water.

I needed to get hold of my doctor. As I turned off the water, the slight burst of energy I enjoyed dwindled to nothing. My thoughts jumbled confusingly, and strange shadows danced in front of my face. Pulling on the sweats and oversized T-shirt I'd been wearing took every bit of energy I possessed.

Still, I struggled and fought and opened the bathroom door. I stared over the seemingly endless expanse of space between myself and my phone and hauled myself toward the coffee table.

Exhausted, out of breath, and struggling every inch of the way, I finally made it to the living room. Grabbing the device, I tried to hold on, but the damn thing tumbled out of my hands and hit the floor. Praying I hadn't shattered my lifeline, I turned it face up. The screen seemed fine, no cracks I could see, but as I hit the button to fire it to life, it flashed and then shut off.

My phone was dead.

I needed help and had no way to reach anyone.

I crawled onto the couch, still tired, listening to *Friends* in the background. I'd been through something like this before. While the symptoms were scary, I made it through then, and I'd make it through now. Tomorrow, I'd schedule an early appointment. Right now, all I had to do was plug in my phone.

I reached for the cord on the side table, using my last stores of strength, and shoved the plug into the phone, praying I'd get the direction, angle, and spot right on the first try. The plug slid home, and I smiled—victorious. Then I closed my eyes again.

CHAPTER EIGHTEEN

ETHAN

I'D DONE what I needed to do with Angie, so why did I feel like crap about how things had ended?

The sound of a vehicle pulling into my driveway dragged my attention out of my head and into the moment. I stood up and walked toward the front door, wondering who might come to visit. A small part hoped that it was Angie, but that was a stupid hope. I'd broken things off with her. I needed to be firm and stick with that decision. My heart might tell me I screwed up, but my brain knew better.

I peeked out the window and saw Bayden's truck. My brother and future sister-in-law headed up the walkway to my front door. Miranda had a familiar bag in her hands, and they both had smiles on their faces. I watched them walk, their voices cheerful as they talked to one another, clearly poking fun and full of love for each other.

Jealous of their joy, I tried to bite back the bitterness filling me. Instead, I pulled open the door and waved at the two of them.

Miranda waved back, but Bayden seemed stuck on something she said and didn't notice me while staring in awe at her.

"How are you holding up?" Miranda's worry filled her features, though her voice stayed upbeat. She obviously knew things were rough between Angie and me, but who told her? I certainly hadn't said a word to anyone. Maybe Patti figured things out in context? Or had Max given something away? I trusted the mail carrier, but I didn't doubt that if he thought I needed help, he'd send the people I could count on most in my direction.

"I'm okay. Who talked?" I put an arm around her shoulders as she pulled me in for a hug. Bayden's gaze met mine, and I could see that *sucks to be you* look in his eyes.

Miranda shrugged as I stepped back and let her inside. "Does somebody need to talk? I mean, this is a small town, and I haven't noticed you at her place or her at yours, so…" She lifted her shoulders another few inches, then lowered them before pressing the bag into my hands.

"What's this?" I asked as Bayden clapped me on the shoulder and headed off toward the bathroom like he owned the place. I expected nothing else from him; family knows to make themselves at home. I motioned to the bag, and Miranda leaned against the kitchen counter.

"Roy's beef stew. You brought me soup when I needed the comfort, and I appreciated that more than I can tell you." She smiled, and I remembered taking the meal over to her place after Bayden asked if I could swing by with something homemade. I whipped up some soup and dropped it off, offering my brother strength to be the man Miranda needed him to be during a rough time.

Touched by her return of the favor and knowing I needed the

support, I opened the bag and breathed in the savory smell of brown gravy.

"Thank you," I said, closing the bag to let it stay warm.

"You're welcome. You can eat it now if you like. We already had ours. Sorry it's not homemade. Who has time for that?" Miranda glanced over at Bayden as he came back into the room. I grabbed a spoon before making my way back to the table and taking a seat.

"Help yourselves," I said, gesturing at the kitchen. "There's milk, beer, tea, coffee, whatever you guys want you're welcome to have."

"We can't stay long." Miranda's cheerful tone didn't inspire worry. "We have another stop to make."

Bayden headed for the sink and grabbed a glass of water, lifting his eyebrows at Miranda, who gave a subtle shake of her head. Their silent communication and the ease and comfort they shared in one another's company again left me envious, and I lowered my head to focus on grabbing a spoonful of Roy's stew.

I wouldn't ask if they had plans or pry into their lives. If they wanted to share what they were up to, they could. If not, then I'd assume whatever they were doing was none of my business.

"How have you been, brother?" Bayden asked as he came over, ruffled my hair annoyingly before taking a seat at the table with me. Miranda lowered herself into another spot, her attention on me. The distinct impression that the pair planned to interrogate me rolled through my thoughts as I took another bite.

"Been better, been worse." Shoving it into my mouth, I enjoyed the richness of the potatoes and beef, the bold herbs and the creamy base. When I swallowed, I turned their questions back on them. "How have you two been?" Besides nauseatingly in love, I meant.

"Fine. When's the last time you talked to Angie?" Miranda's curious tone should've annoyed me—I didn't like people trying to pry into my business—but I sighed instead.

"Look, I told her off yesterday. She's uh, been keeping some secrets I can't agree with." I held up a hand to stop them from talking over me. "While I'm disappointed with her decisions, I'm also not going to gossip about what those secrets are." I wouldn't share her actions, though I disagreed with them.

Miranda glanced at Bayden. "You already know everything, then?" The confusion in her features didn't surprise me. No doubt whatever Angie told them about her reason for being here didn't match what she told me. It was her inability to be honest that ruined everything.

I nodded. "I do. I was the first to know." I took another bite of food, refusing to look at either of them. "I'm still not going to discuss anything." I'd given her my word that I wouldn't gossip about her, and I planned to keep it.

"Okay." Miranda stood up and headed for the door.

"We'll talk to you later, okay, brother?" Bayden stood and clapped me on the shoulder. "Call us if you need anything."

"Try to remember, sometimes people hide things to protect themselves or protect their image. People want us to see them a certain way, and vulnerability isn't exactly comfortable. I know that firsthand. Have a good day, Ethan." Miranda's soft voice had me turning away to keep her from seeing the knife twisting in my gut at her words.

The pair left, and I sat, finishing the food in front of me, though now the delicious dish tasted like nothing more than cardboard. Angie had told Miranda and Bayden her secrets, and they'd taken her freaking side.

I folded my hands together, planted my elbows on the table, and stared into space while I chewed.

Sometimes people hide things to protect themselves or protect their image. People want us to see them a certain way, and vulnerability isn't exactly comfortable.

Did that excuse her actions? Still, knowing that Bayden and Miranda had forgiven her so quickly—and I hadn't—bothered me.

I finished the stew and carried the container to the fridge. Putting away the leftovers for later, I washed my plate, realizing that I no longer found comfort in being here alone. The silence somehow sounded overwhelming and seeing Bayden and Miranda happy together and in sync made me ache for what Angie and I had.

Or what she made me believe we had.

The sound of her laugh filled my ears, and flashes of her danced through my thoughts. The playful way she ducked behind the sheet, covering our heads and giggling when I pulled her in for a kiss after we made love. The sweet tone of her voice as she talked, the way her lightheartedness instantly picked up my spirits...

I missed her.

I missed the memories we'd been making, the closeness we shared, all the funny texts and playful jokes back and forth. Picking up my phone, I touched the messages, then her name. Our previous conversation popped up, and a bitter ache swept through me, tightening my stomach.

What are you saying, exactly? She'd asked me.

I'm saying that I'm done. Whatever you manufactured between us, it's over.

She hadn't responded, but what was there to say? I told her we were through. No room for conversation, no opportunity to discuss ... *done*. What kind of response could she give?

I sank to the couch, more defeated than I had ever felt before, and wondered if I made the wrong choice. Angie had been under my skin since the day I met her. What made me think I could get her out now. Especially after that night—the night we made love. And it was love because nothing had ever felt that honest in my existence.

CHAPTER NINETEEN

ANGIE

SOMEONE KNOCKED AT THE DOOR, and I called out for them to come in while I stayed curled in a ball on the couch. I'd woken up feeling better than I had the day before, but only somewhat. I knew I couldn't drive, and I wouldn't risk anyone else's life trying. I waited as long as I could before realizing things weren't magically going to get better.

I did the next thing I could think of; I called the sheriff—Miranda, Ethan's brother's wife, who said she'd be over after a quick stop.

Terrible idea, maybe, but what other choice did I have? I couldn't call Roy after my embarrassing stunt accusing him of being my dad. I didn't doubt he'd help, but I didn't have the energy to face him. I knew I could trust Miranda, and she was the sheriff. I mean, protect and serve, right? Plus, I knew they were good people.

The knob turned, and Miranda walked in, her features

worried as she came up to me. "How are you?" she asked, not glancing at Bayden, who stayed right on her heels.

"You look terrible," Bayden said.

"Thanks a lot. You're a real charmer." I smiled, not insulted by his words and still strong enough to call him out for being rude.

"Sorry," he said, but I shook my head. I preferred the humor and honesty over being treated like some delicate, breakable object people needed to handle gently.

"Like I said, it's not an emergency, I promise." I watched them both look me up and down, their expressions not agreeing. "I need you to please take me to that address I texted. I can give you gas money for the ride, but I can't drive right now or that might be an emergency."

Miranda held up a hand. "You don't owe us anything. Let's just get you over there, okay? Don't stress about a thing."

I nodded, appreciative of her support but still determined to pay them back. I'm not a freeloader, and I don't take advantage of people.

"Can you walk?" Miranda perched on the couch next to me, and I let out a nervous chuckle.

"Maybe?" Weakness and fatigue ruled my body, and it was all I could do to stay awake. Walking might be an impossibility.

Miranda glanced at Bayden, who nodded. She stood and moved away, and Bayden leaned in. "I'm sorry about this," he said, carefully scooping me up.

I clung to him as Miranda spoke.

"Do you have an emergency bag?" she asked.

I nodded. "In my trunk. My keys are hanging in the kitchen."

She hurried off as Bayden carried me toward the front door.

"Sorry if I'm heavy." My nerves were acting up, and I wasn't used to people carrying me. The last person to carry me had been Ethan, and that memory stung. My cheeks blazed, and Bayden let out a snort.

"You're light as a feather." He transported me to the truck, easily opening the door with me in his arms. With a gentle motion, he deposited me neatly in the seat as Miranda closed my trunk and returned with my overnight bag slung over her shoulder.

"I'll lock up." Miranda held up my keys. "Your house key is on this, right?" I nodded as Bayden pulled the seat belt across my shoulder and clicked it home before walking around to the driver's seat and turning up the heat.

"Are you warm enough?" he asked as Miranda hurried back and climbed inside.

"Yes, thank you. I really appreciate this, you guys." My throat closed up, and I struggled to keep back tears.

"No problem." Miranda blew me off as Bayden pulled out of my driveway. I noticed the truck smelled like woodchips and sawdust, a country mix that felt like home.

I hated feeling like a burden, and I despised inconveniencing them. "I'm sorry to ruin your plans today." I glanced out the window as we drove down the street before turning onto Main and nosing toward the highway to Silver Springs.

"You ruined nothing." Bayden smiled at Miranda, and her hand found his. I smiled at their adorableness, my heart aching as I thought about Ethan.

"I bet if you had asked Ethan, he would have driven you." Miranda's nonchalant tone put me at ease.

"We're not exactly talking right now." I didn't know what he'd told them, but I wasn't about to talk badly about him or give them too many details.

"I'm sorry." Miranda's understanding voice brought tears to my eyes. "Relationships are tough."

"I do appreciate your kindness," I said, feeling indebted to these two.

"Stop thanking us. This is the right thing to do, and it's not a big deal." Bayden's words might be harsh, but his warm tone took all the sting out of them.

"It's a big deal to me." My words were little more than a whisper; I couldn't do better around the aching lump in my throat. Against my will, my eyes drifted closed again.

"Hey, we're here, hon." Miranda stood at my door before Bayden moved her aside. I bolted upright, releasing my seat belt as I tried to remember where I was—Bayden's truck. I glanced around. Silver Springs ... my treatment center.

Without a word, Bayden scooped me up again, and I noticed Miranda's worried glance before she met my gaze with a calm smile.

As he carried me to the door, I saw a familiar vehicle and a familiar face. What the heck? Why was Max at the dialysis treatment center in Silver Springs?

I couldn't make sense of seeing the man, and his stare told me he didn't expect to see me. The surprise in his features warned that he wasn't there for me.

The automatic doors slid open, and Bayden carried me to the front desk. The lady leaped to her feet, a stunned expression in her eyes. "Angie?"

"Hi, Macy," I whispered.

"Where do we take her?" Bayden asked.

Macy lifted her white brows, her eyes widening as she studied me. "To the hospital, honey. She has jaundice and has lost far too much weight. She needs more care than we can give her here."

Without a word, Bayden circled around to carry me out. Miranda thanked the woman as I tried to make sense of what she said. Why wouldn't they treat me? I booked an appointment. I'd come to the treatment center. What problem did they have?

Moments later, loaded back up and leaving the parking lot, Miranda glanced at me. "Want me to call Ethan?"

I shook my head. "I don't want to bother him."

She and Bayden shared a look.

"Please, just take me and drop me off." I felt terrible having asked them to bring me here only to have to take more of their time because these guys wouldn't see me.

"We can stay with you if you like. It's no trouble at all." Miranda smiled back at me, but I shook my head. I wouldn't take up any more of their time than I already had.

As Bayden pulled into the hospital complex and followed the signs to the ER, my anxiety rose. I hated hospitals.

I waited for him to park, unbuckled my belt, desperate to stand on my own and walk into the hospital. Opening the door, I slid out of the seat onto the concrete, my knees buckling the second I tried to put weight on them. In a flash, Bayden appeared and scooped me into his arms, leaving me uncomfortable as Miranda closed the door and walked beside us, my overnight bag slung over her shoulder.

I packed that stupid bag in case something like this ever happened, but I never used it before and didn't think I'd ever have to. Now I found myself glad I packed it.

Bayden settled me into a wheelchair and wheeled me to the front window to check in. In moments, they ushered me back to triage, and I waved goodbye to Miranda and Bayden.

"You have our number," Miranda said, obviously getting the message that I didn't want them to stay any longer than necessary.

"I'll call with my room number as soon as I can." At that moment, I accepted I wouldn't be going home soon.

They nodded, watching as the nurse wheeled me out of sight. I answered the questions I could, held still while they drew blood, ran tests, poked, prodded, and looked me over. Too weak to fight, I just let them do whatever they wanted, and my mind drifted back to Ethan's smile. The kind light in his eyes, and the warmth of his affection.

And the second the medical staff left me in peace, I drifted to sleep.

"Angie?"

I blinked at the doctor.

"I'm Dr. Michael. I hear you're not feeling too well today." His calm tone didn't put me at ease as the nurse filed in behind him to take my blood pressure and fuss with my IV.

"I'm in terrible shape, aren't I?" I didn't want him to be nice. I wanted to know the cold, hard facts. As I watched his face, I knew the news would be difficult to hear. He sat down on his little rolling stool and scooted up to take a closer look at me. I didn't know him, but I recognized the worry in his eyes.

"I'm afraid so." His salt-and-pepper hair and fine lines gave him a fatherly air, and my whole soul cried out for that paternal comfort.

"We have your medical history, so we knew which tests to run. It looks like you have uremia and renal failure. Do you know what that means?" His soft voice hit me like an asteroid, and my heart sank. I knew exactly what that meant, and it wasn't good.

"I thought I'd have more time." I didn't know what else to say as the nurse offered me a weak smile.

"I'm sorry. We're going to keep you for treatment and put you on the transplant list—"

"But there's like a five-year waiting list." I knew the likelihood of a transplant wasn't great. Many people need transplants and never get them. There was a good chance that I'd never walk out of here.

"Right now, your kidneys are failing. You have an excess of urea in the blood, which you know is bad. Urea belongs in your urine. Your kidneys are not working to remove waste products, and that's why you're so tired and feel so awful. We'll do everything in our power to help your body function until we can get that transplant for you. That means transferring you out of the ER." The terror rose in my throat. They were preparing for long term. I didn't want to be admitted and stuck in the hospital for the foreseeable future, but I also didn't want to die.

He put his stethoscope in his ears and pressed the cold end under my gown against my chest and listened. "Thankfully, your heart sounds good, no abnormal rhythm."

"I'm not going home, am I?" I stared at him, noting his hesitation before he spoke.

"Not today, but we'll do everything we can to make sure you get there, okay?"

I lowered my head to the pillow and stared up into the bright lights. The door slid open, and a woman poked her head in. "She has a visitor."

"Do you have questions for me?" the doctor asked.

I shook my head as twin tears escaped the corners of my eyes and rolled toward the pillow.

"We'll move you in a few moments, okay?"

I nodded, and he shuffled out with the nurse right behind him as someone came in and closed the heavy door.

"Hey, kiddo, how are you doing?" Max's voice filled the air.

"Did you follow us?" Despite my surprise that he'd shown up, I couldn't process anything.

"I did, and I'm sorry. I don't want to breach your personal space, but we need to talk."

I had no idea what he wanted to discuss, but he was welcome to say whatever was on his mind.

"Go ahead." It wasn't like I could get out of this bed. I knew I'd be trapped in the hospital until they could find me a donor. "I'm all ears."

"Angie, do you have polycystic kidney disease?"

I lifted my head and glanced at him.

"How did you know?"

He frowned. "Please don't be mad at Ethan for confiding in me. He needed someone to talk to, and I swear I didn't tell anyone else, but I'm glad he told me you weren't feeling well because I think you're my daughter." He walked up to my side and took my hand.

Frozen, I stared up at him. "You're my dad?"

He smiled. "Yes, I think I am."

"I'm scared." The past fell away, and my heart spoke the words that my head couldn't wrap around. "They say I need a kidney transplant."

With that, he hugged me. "It's going to be okay."

Everything swirled in my mind. "You're my father?" Nothing made sense, and yet it did.

"I swear I didn't know your mom got pregnant. What we had was not planned, and then it happened and she left. Then I left. I had no idea."

I nodded. "I know."

"I would've been there if I'd known."

I didn't doubt him for one second. "I'm glad you found me." Funny, I set out in search of my father, but my father found me instead.

He pulled up a chair and sat beside me, his hand still on mine. "My wife..." he choked up, and I stared at him, stunned. I hadn't known about his wife. "She donated her kidney to me a long time ago." His eyes teared up, and I wanted to hug him.

"She saved my life, but there was a complication, and she passed away. I never thought the trade-off was worth it. I should've died and she should've lived, you know?"

"You've honored her memory by living well and being kind." My heart went out to him. Max, the unofficial dad of Cross Creek, the man everyone could count on, the keeper of secrets, the kindest person I ever met ... he deserved to live.

He nodded his head, staring down at the floor. "I've tried. I wish I could give you mine, but—"

"I know." He couldn't.

"I'm sorry I wasn't there for you. I apologize for not figuring it out sooner. I saw you at the clinic and it all clicked." He breathed a sigh. "I volunteer there every week offering snacks and drinks but usually on Monday."

"I get treatment every Tuesday. Or I did." We'd been so close but missed each other every week.

The door opened, and a nurse peeked in. "Sorry to interrupt, but we need to move her now."

My father nodded, then glanced at me again, a slight, sad smile curving the corners of his lips. "I'm not going anywhere."

CHAPTER TWENTY

ETHAN

MY PHONE RANG, and Max's voice filled the silence. "Ethan, you need to listen to me."

The only reason I picked up the call was because I was curious why he'd interrupt my pity party for one. His serious tone bolted me upright. What made him sound wound up?

"I'm listening." I held my breath, wondering what the hell would come out of his mouth. I had zero doubt whatever he said next would be important.

"Angie is my daughter."

I took the news like a surprise right hook to the face, slouching on my couch in stunned silence. Max? Her father was Max? She'd been looking for *him* all this time, and he'd been right there. How had they not known? Did she have something to do with the wife he never discussed? She said her mother wasn't nice. He couldn't imagine Max staying with a woman like that.

He broke my thoughts up with more talk.

"She's in the hospital right now with kidney failure."

My stomach twisted in knots as I struggled to make sense of his insane words. Angie was in the hospital? Kidney failure? What the hell?

"Wait, what?" I needed him to slow down and explain.

"Remember the drugs you saw her taking? She suffers from polycystic kidney disease, the same illness I have." His fast-flowing words didn't make sense. "It's hereditary, and I passed it down to her."

"The pills in her medicine cabinet?" I got so confused. If she'd been sick enough that she needed to be in the hospital, how could I have missed that? I thought about how sick she was the last day I saw her and felt awful. She should've been in the hospital then, and I was too blinded by anger to notice.

"You know she's sick, but she's a lot sicker than you thought." Max's voice held the same shock that filled me.

Numb with confusion, I leaned forward as helplessness washed over me. It was the same feeling I had the day my father passed away. Now Angie sat in a hospital, possibly dying, and I hadn't known anything about her either.

"Where are you at?"

"Silver Springs, and Ethan, you need to remember that Angie is not your father." Something in Max's voice broke. "I promise this isn't a jab at you, but she didn't know how bad of shape she was in when Miranda and Bayden brought her in."

Miranda and Bayden took her in? The weight of that crushed my soul. She hadn't called me because I told her we were through. I hadn't been there when she needed me like I hadn't been there for my father.

"Did Miranda and Bayden know when they stopped by?" I rethought our entire conversation and realized that they must not have been talking about mine and Angie's break up or the reason she was in Cross Creek. They were asking if I knew how sick she was without actually asking. I stood and paced, shoving a hand through my hair. *Damn it.*

"You'd have to ask them. I'm here with her right now. She's sleeping, but they have her hooked up to all kinds of machines."

"Will she be okay?" Dumb question, but I needed to know the answer.

Max sighed. "She's in trouble and needs a kidney transplant." The fear in his voice shook me to my core.

The thought of my father flashed in my mind. "I wasn't there for my dad and now this."

"You were. He knew you had his back until the very end. This isn't like that. She didn't know she was this sick." Max paused. "Most people live their entire lives with this illness, well into their sixties before it becomes life-threatening."

"She hid it from me." We'd been building a relationship, and I'd been falling for her. And after what I'd been through with my father's illness and death—

"Did you tell her about your dad?"

His words stopped me short, and I shook my head. My voice followed a second later. "I didn't."

"She had no way of knowing that you needed to know this, or how important it was that she not hide an illness from you. Ethan, she's a young woman. Has she ever wanted you to see her as vulnerable or weak?" He made sense, but my brain swirled.

"No, but—"

"Do you think she wanted you to see her as sick or fragile?"

"No, but Max, I should've known. Not only about her illness, but her whole reason for being here. Hell, she secretly tested my brothers' and my hair to see if we were related."

"Ethan, she did what she thought she had to do. Check your ego at the door. She's not perfect. You're not perfect. But I know you care for her. I'd even go so far as to say that I think you could fall in love with her if you could forgive her human imperfections." Max's tone resonated in me, and I knew he was right.

I could fall in love with Angie if I could look past my damn insecurities. If I could find compassion for the tough spot life put her in and get over myself and the things life put me through. Yes, I could love her.

I hesitated. "What happens if she doesn't get the transplant?" I needed to step up and be there for Angie and Max during this hard time.

"She stays in the hospital where they can keep her blood clean until they can find a match." Max sounded sad, and he had a tone of finality.

"How long will that take?" I held my breath.

"Weeks? Months? Years? There's no telling." Max sounded like he'd given up. "I'd give her my kidney if I could, but I can't. Remember my wife? She gave me her kidney and lost her life because of it. I struggle with that every day. Dammit, I don't want to lose her when I just found her." His words tore at me, and I suddenly saw the situation for what it was. Max had discovered his daughter in time to potentially watch her die. If nothing else, he'd have to watch her suffer.

"I need to go, Max. I'm sorry, but I've got something to do. There are wrongs I need to make right." With that, I hung up the phone, left my house, and drove to the hospital. Each time my phone rang, I ignored it. No one could talk me out of what I planned to do.

My mother raised me to do the right thing.

My father raised me to be a good man.

I could imagine both of them now, reminding me who they nurtured me to be, what they taught me, and telling me to be the man they raised me to be.

"I miss you, Dad," I said, watching the world slip by on the way to Silver Springs.

My mind ran wild. Her hair appointment hadn't been the reason she didn't want me to go. It had been a front for treatment. I thought about the weight she'd lost. The sadness in her eyes. Her desperation to find her father. What if she'd been desperate to find him for answers? What if there were other medical issues she needed to know? What if she'd been hanging on, hoping to find a donor who could give her a second chance at life?

With both hands on the wheel, I sped along the highway. Maybe she hoped for a sibling willing to be her donor. I'd been unfair to her. My phone continued to ring, but I didn't give a damn. I was on a mission.

Angie might have been dealing with the most challenging time of her life, and I hadn't had a forgiving bone in my body for her. My dad would be so disappointed. My mother would yell at me if she knew the complete story. Shame filled me to the brim as I took the exit with the big blue H sign.

I followed the arrows, my memory slipping back to my father, to his warm voice and bright eyes. He'd been such a good person, and he taught me to take care of others when I could—to be the bigger man. To step up and step in when someone needed help. I couldn't think of a better way to honor his memory than to do those things.

I pulled into the hospital lot and parked. Within twenty minutes, I got my blood drawn. "We'll see if you're a match, Mr. Lockhart."

I answered the questions, gave info, signed consent forms, and watched the lab tech flirt with the guy next to her. She gathered up my vials and went on to the next patient. The whole time, Max's voice was in my ear.

I'd give her my kidney if I could... I don't want to lose her when I just found her.

Nobody deserved that pain. Not Max, not me when I lost my father, no one. Loss, when it was inevitable, was soul-crushing. Loss, when it could be prevented ... that was heartbreaking. I wouldn't let her go when I could potentially single-handedly save her life.

I would honor my father's memory and make my mother proud.

And Angie ... I would do my best to give her the gift of life. What she did with that gift ... that was up to her.

CHAPTER TWENTY-ONE

ANGIE

THE BEEP of monitors and the quiet sound of my breathing were all I heard. Every inhale, every exhale sounded louder than the strongest storm in my ears, and I remembered why I always hated hospital rooms.

The lights were too bright, though someone had thoughtfully dimmed them. The sharp scent of the sterile room burned my nose. The chill where the IV fluid entered the back of my hand left my arm aching. The thin blankets did nothing to warm me, and the hum of the dialysis machine was like a song I loathed and loved at the same time. Hospitals were places that held hundreds of people, but you felt so alone.

Luck and time weren't on my side, but panicking, stressing, and allowing fear to rule my head and heart wouldn't help either.

A slight sound to my right, a sniff, maybe, told me I wasn't actually alone like I thought. Someone kept a silent vigil nearby—or nearly silent, anyway—and my heart called out for Ethan.

Rolling my head sideways, I caught sight of Max sitting

forward in the chair, his elbows on his knees, and his gaze fixed on the floor between his feet. His defeated posture left me with little doubt about the shape I was in.

Despite the initial flash of disappointment that Ethan wasn't here, I breathed a sigh of relief. Max was my father, and I finally found him after so much searching. Life was cruel to let me find him, only to lose him.

"Hello," I whispered to let him know I was awake.

He lifted his head, a slight smile tugging the corners of his lips. "Well, hello there. Did you sleep well?"

I thought about my rest for a moment, trying to remember exactly when I'd fallen asleep and came up empty. The all-consuming blackness hadn't contained dreams. At some point, I closed my eyes, and time leaped forward to opening them again. "I think so."

I wanted to thank him for staying with me, for being here when I woke up, for being the dad I needed because I sure as heck couldn't call my mom and tell her I was in the hospital. She made it clear that my health issues were my own doing because she refused to admit that I had an inherited illness, a genetic gift—erm, a *curse* from the father she lied about all my life.

"I'm glad you're here." I slid my arm off the bed toward him. Max scooted his chair in my direction to close the gap between us, reached out, and took my hand in both of his. With his warm fingers wrapped comfortably around mine, we sat in silence for a few moments as a sense of foreboding filled me. I didn't have much time, and I wanted to know everything.

"Tell me about yourself."

He studied me a moment, then inhaled. "I was a quiet kid. My mom said I never cried, and that freaked her out. While I was teething, all I did was drool like mad and chew on everything I could get my hands on, but I didn't cry."

I smiled, thinking of him as a tiny baby wrapped in his mother's loving embrace.

"As I got older, I grew interested in cars and, no joke, the postal service. As a kid, I loved stories of the Pony Express and decided I wanted to be a mailman."

I smiled, loving the thought that he'd always known who he was and what he'd be. "That's cute."

He chuckled. "As a kid, I'd ride my horse hard and pretend I was part of the Pony Express, delivering mail from imaginary friends and important people like the President." His eyes softened as he thought about the past, and I imagined him as a kid delivering imaginary mail with that light in his eyes. "You grew up with horses?" I asked, envying his upbringing. Or that part of his childhood, at least.

He nodded. "I was raised on a farm. My parents expected me to take it over when I grew up, but that didn't happen." Sadness took over, and I wondered what story he held back. I didn't have to wait long to find out. "When I got sick, they didn't know what to think. In the end, they wound up selling the farm to pay for my medical bills."

I squeezed his fingers gently, offering silent support and reassurance. "I'm sorry." This illness ... it wasn't kind. It came with the ability to steal everything from us, our health, money, time, heck, even friendships and family.

He nodded. "Thank you."

"I bet they are proud you grew into a man that followed his dreams." He might not see how inspiring of a man he'd become, but I could see that. After all, this illness had stolen many dreams from me. I couldn't begin to explain how difficult delivering mail had to be for him on bad days, yet he never missed work.

"They passed away when I was a young man—in my twenties. A drunk driver hit them when they were crossing the street after going dancing on their anniversary." His throat bobbed as he swallowed, and his eyes took on the sheen of tears.

"I'm sorry."

He studied my face. "That was around the time I met your mother. I came here looking for peace. She arrived looking for fun. I was making bad choices at the height of grief. I knew instantly we weren't right for one another, but things just happened. She left before I knew about you, and she never told me. I went back home to Southern Colorado and life went on. I'm so sorry."

I shrugged. "I don't fault you. Going through such a tough time, I mean, I imagine finding solace anywhere after that tragedy isn't a bad thing." I thought about how the world stopped while Ethan held me in his arms. I considered how he could make my troubles, doubts, and fears all melt away. I understood why my father looked for comfort in the arms of another person. That connection was powerful.

After all, if Ethan sat here right now, I'd be hugging him and begging him not to let go.

"I found my wife not long after."

I perked up, curious about this story. Did I have half-siblings?

"She lit my life up, and I loved her more than I thought possible. We dated, shared interests, and she made me happy. When I got sick, she gave me her kidney." He inhaled, and there was a slight shudder in the sound that sent my heart plummeting.

"Tell me everything. Tell me what happened to her."

He talked in a lower, throatier voice as if his windpipe

suddenly collapsed. "She, uh, made it through the surgery." With another long inhale, he struggled to hold himself together, and I squeezed his hand tighter to remind him that I was there for him.

"There was a complication, and she developed a blood clot and suffered a stroke and passed away." His unsteady voice dropped to a whisper. "It happened so quickly."

My heart ached for him, and I grabbed his hand with my other hand, pulling on the IV and dialysis tubes. I adjusted to get a better grip and held on to him as if I could squeeze the pain away. "I'm sorry, Max."

I couldn't imagine losing Ethan like that, though I knew I'd already lost him. That thought sent agony rippling through me, and I clung to Max silently, wishing our pain could evaporate. Why did life have to be so difficult and excruciating? Why did bad things happen to good people?

"I messed things up with Ethan." I blurted the words, hating myself for making the moment about me, but Max seemed relieved. "I'm sorry, I wasn't trying to make this about me."

"It's okay, I don't talk about this much. It's painful, and I said enough."

That he shared something with me he didn't talk about much touched me.

"What happened with Ethan?" He scooted in closer, and I adjusted, rolling partially toward him as the cuff tightened to recheck my blood pressure.

"I hid my illness from him and didn't tell him why I came to Cross Creek. I even stole hair samples to eliminate Kip from my list. I screwed everything up." I stared at our hands.

"Can I tell you a secret?" he asked, leaning in a bit and speaking in a whisper.

I nodded, letting out a short laugh.

"I'm not sure secrets are good."

He chuckled. "I'd agree, but I've been talking to him about your relationship. He told me everything. The reason he's so sensitive about you keeping something a secret is because his dad had a heart problem and told no one. He sees every secret as a betrayal."

I inhaled a deep breath as things made more sense.

"He's not a fan of any kind of omission. However, I understand your reasons, and I tried to talk some sense into him. I don't know if it worked, though." He let out a sigh. "That boy is as hard-headed as they come."

I couldn't hold back a smile at his accurate assessment of Ethan. "I know, but I messed up. I should've been honest with him." A spiny lump pricked my throat as tears filled my eyes. I messed everything up, and it cost me the man I'd been falling in love with.

Not that I'd complain; now Max and I were making up for lost time, discussing things we'd missed in one another's lives, and I felt like I knew him better now than I ever had.

Time wasn't on my side. I could make peace with that, though there was much I wished I could do. "I pray he'll forgive me."

"I'm sure he has. He's not a perfect person either." Max's sad voice brought me some relief.

"I swear I intended no harm to come to him through all of this." I hadn't masterminded some plot to hurt the Lockhart brothers, especially not Ethan.

Max patted my hand. "I know, I know. You have a good heart, Angie."

His absolute acceptance filled me with warmth, and I rested my head back on the pillows, staring up at the white speckled tiles.

If my time to go had come, I'd do my best to face that end with honor, grace, and dignity.

"Thank you for being here. For not making me do this alone. It means a lot to me."

"Thank you for allowing me to be by your side, and I'm sorry I haven't been there all along. You're an amazing woman, and I'm proud of who you've become." His tone told me he meant every word.

My dad was proud of me. How long had I been waiting to find that validation and unconditional love?

Far too long.

The part that hurt the worst was knowing I found him too late.

CHAPTER TWENTY-TWO

ETHAN

"I'M SORRY, sir, but you're not a match." The tech's face emitted sympathy and calm, though I found myself wound up tighter than I'd ever been in my life. I stood in the little lab as the walls squeezed in, and realization came. I rushed through all the tests requesting to be an anonymous donor to Angie, only to be turned away.

Numb, I sat down in an uncomfortable chair with a wooden-looking frame and blue Naugahyde-upholstered cushion in the waiting area.

"Are you sure I'm not a match? I mean, I don't think the lab tech was paying attention." I'd been so sure that this would go well. It all played out in my mind. I'd come in here, they'd take my kidney, and give Angie a new chance at life. Instead, the option had been cruelly stripped away, leaving me helpless to do anything for her.

The dark-haired tech touched his blue surgical mask with a gloved hand. His white garb helped him blend into the over-bright lights in the room, and I wondered how the young woman behind the counter wrote anything down, much less worked on her computer.

"I'm sorry. You're still welcome to donate, but it'll go to someone else who needs it." The tech's eyes crinkled at the corners, and I knew he was smiling at me, no doubt trying to comfort me and forgetting about the mask on his face.

"I'll think about it." I wasn't against donating a kidney, but the shock of learning I couldn't donate it to Angie hadn't worn off.

"Take all the time you need," the tech said before giving the young blonde behind the white counter a significant stare. She smiled, and he headed into the back room while she bent her head and continued whatever she'd been working on.

Max's voice still rang in my ears. *I'd give her my kidney if I could... I don't want to lose her when I just found her.*

The words were heavier than the bags of concrete I'd thrown around with my brothers in happier times. More crushing than the time when Bayden and I were teens working on his truck when the tire rim had fused to the studs but finally popped free landing on my foot. I failed Angie, and I failed Max, and the sense of hopelessness that accompanied that thought left me breathless and aching.

I put my elbows on my knees, my head in my hands, and stared at the speckled, cream-colored flooring. What else was there to do but call Max and tell him the news?

Taking a breath, I pulled out my phone. Through a slight blur of tears, I called him. The line rang several times, and when he finally answered, he sounded out of breath. "Hello?"

"I'm sorry. I tried." Miserable, I prepared myself for what I knew would be a tough conversation.

"Tried what, Ethan? What's going on?" His confusion cut me to the quick, and I knew I needed to explain. I never told him my plan. Maybe that had turned out to be a blessing of sorts. Not telling him meant he hadn't told Angie, which meant she didn't have the chance to get her hopes up only to be dashed by what I'd tell Max next.

"I came in to see if I was a match and if I could donate my kidney to Angie." My throat ached, and no more words could squeeze through as my failure pushed down on my shoulders with enough force that they felt ready to break.

Max said nothing for a moment.

"You were going to give her your kidney?" There was pride and concern in his voice, but it didn't overshadow the sadness. "You would do that even after what I told you?"

He meant the death of his wife and that had crossed my mind, but losing your life in the quest to save another was honorable.

"Yes. When you care for someone, none of the risks matter. Besides, this is what my father would've wanted me to do, regardless of how her and my relationship turned out." As I said the words, I knew they weren't the only reason I wanted to donate my kidney to Angie. "Helping her is the right thing to do."

"What happened?"

"They said we're not a match, but Max, I swear they're wrong. I feel it in my gut. Angie and I are the perfect match in everything. It makes little sense." I hated letting Max down, but I'd done my best.

Max let out a huff. "They didn't tell us that there was a donor." I could hear him in the background, talking to a nurse, but couldn't make out what he was saying. Waiting patiently, I sat back in my seat, studying the plain white walls around me. The hospital's architecture had always fascinated me, but this little lab left much to be desired despite the front wall made of steel and glass.

"Are you still at the lab?" Max asked.

"Yeah, why?" What was he up to?

"Stay put." His muffled voice continued talking to someone else, and I tried not to be annoyed he hadn't answered my question of *why* he wanted to know.

Instead, he asked me a suspiciously familiar question. "Are you O positive or negative?"

"I'm positive."

"Excellent, what about drugs or alcohol?"

"You know me better than that. I drink a beer here and there but no drugs." I wanted to know what he was up to.

I adjusted in the uncomfortable seat as the blonde behind the counter cradled the phone between her cheek and shoulder and stared at me.

"Have you taken any medications like aspirin, ibuprofen, or blood thinners in the last week?" I recognized the questions that the technicians had already asked me. Questions that made no sense for Max to be asking me now.

"No. Not even Tylenol for a headache." I avoided medications unless I absolutely needed them. If a job left me sore, I stretched, worked out, or took a hot shower. Medications were the last resort.

He continued talking to someone else, and I stood up to pace the room. Blondie glanced up at me, her blue eyes following my progress before she shuffled her papers and started typing away at her computer.

"Am I bothering you?" I asked her quietly, tilting the cell phone away from my ear so Max wouldn't think I was asking him.

She shook her head with a slight smile before returning to her work.

"Are you going to come up and see her?" Max asked.

I pushed open the door and headed out into the fresh, chilly air. "I'm not sure if that's a good idea."

"Will you be able to forgive yourself if you don't?" Max's honest question stirred something within me, and I paced back and forth in front of the lab.

Could I forgive myself if I didn't say goodbye when I had the chance? What if she passed away and I never said another word to her?

I needed to apologize. There were plenty of things I needed to say that, if I didn't say them soon, I might never get another chance. What if she didn't want to see me? What if she—rightfully—hated me?

"I don't want to pressure you, but she told me she wanted you to forgive her." Max's soft voice told me he understood but thought I should step up and maybe he was right.

"I need to get back in there and check on her. Talk to you again soon."

As we said our goodbyes and hung up, I struggled to come to terms with the facts. The woman I could love—did love—perched on the edge of death. My attempt to save her life and give her my kidney had failed, and this might be my last chance to tell her I was sorry for being cruel, for breaking up with her—it was my time to make peace.

The more I thought about everything, the more I realized there wasn't any question about what I should do.

I turned to head toward her room but heard someone say my name. Pivoting around, I noticed the blonde waving me down.

"Ethan Lockhart, right?" She glanced at the papers in her hands.

My mouth went dry. "Yeah, that's me."

"You wanted to donate a kidney to Angie Sutton?" Her gaze locked on me before darting back to the papers in her hand.

"Yes, I'm not a match."

"We re-ran the information because of a call from her doctor. There was a mistake in the blood typing. Actually, it was my mistake." She lowered her head as she thumbed through the sheets in her hand. "It was my mistake. I got distracted and typed in the wrong blood type for you. I'm sorry."

My heart thrashed against my ribs like ocean waves in a wicked storm. *They'd made a mistake?*

Her gaze met mine, and a smile crossed her lips. "Mr. Lockhart, you're a match. Are you ready to save a life?"

I'd never been more ready for anything.

CHAPTER TWENTY-THREE

ANGIE

I WONDERED what Ethan was doing that minute. I could see him in my mind, tablet in hand, gaze glued to the screen, his fingers tracing lines, and his brilliant mind constantly calculating numbers.

As the surrounding machines hummed and whirred, I smiled at the thought of the man I fell for. So many times, I wished him to be by my side, but a girl only got so many wishes, and I was at my quota—I got my father.

The scratchy hospital sheet under me and thin blankets over me were as far from home as I could get, and I wanted to be anywhere but here.

Staring at the door, I wondered where Max had run off to.

The phone rang, and I reached for the oversized handheld with the enormous buttons, surprised that anyone had corded phones anymore. "Hello?" I had no idea who might call or why because I hadn't let anyone else know where I was except Bayden and Miranda. I couldn't imagine them telling anyone without asking me first.

"Hey, how are you?" Roy's gentle voice, along with Gypsy's in the background, brought a smile to my face. "Max called and let us know you were here."

Of course, Max would because he was a good man.

I readjusted, trying to get more comfortable as the endless shuffle of blood running from one arm into the machine to be cleaned and back into my arm left me struggling to relax. "I've been better. Not complaining, though."

"We're thinking about you." Roy's voice quickly faded as Gypsy talked over him. "Want us to come to visit?"

"Sure, I'm in room three sixteen. Will you bring Max some food? He's had a hospital lunch, but it's garbage. I'll pay you." My worry for Max had settled like a cement block in my gut. This whole difficult situation was more than I wanted to put anyone through, much less someone I cared about.

"Of course, and no charge. We're family helping family." Roy's statement reminded me of the news I wanted to tell, but first, I needed Max's permission. I didn't want to tell the world and blindside him in the process.

"Thank you." As the words left my lips, some weight eased off my shoulders and chest, allowing me to breathe easier.

Gypsy spoke. "Give us about thirty minutes, and then we'll be there. Big hugs and much love, Angie."

I said my goodbyes, and we hung up, leaving me feeling more loved than ever. As restless as I felt, and as much as I wanted out of the hospital, a sense of duty compelled me to stay and see this through. Going home meant going to hospice, as my failing kidneys couldn't support my life without dialysis or a donor.

No matter how badly I wanted to rip the tubes out of my arms and make a break for it, I owed the people in my life my best. For them, I'd fight until I exhausted all options.

Turning my head toward the window, I exhaled. That didn't mean I wouldn't give anything to feel the sunlight on my face or the chilly winter air on my skin or inhale the crisp, sharp scent of snow. I'd give almost anything to enjoy the smell of an evergreen tree dressed in twinkling lights and glass bulbs, or taste Roy's garlic knots, or feel Ethan's arms around me.

"You're a million miles away."

I jumped, unaware that Max had come back into the room. Offering him a tired smile, I opted for the simple truth. "I don't want to be here. I'm wondering if I'll ever enjoy the simple pleasures like the crunch of fresh snow under my shoes, the laugh after slipping crazily on ice, or the ability to call a friend when I'm in trouble." Every option included a memory of Ethan; the way his shoes packed down the snow when we walked into Roy's, the way he grabbed my arm to keep me from falling on the sidewalk, and the way he drove out to save me when my car drifted into that snowbank.

Tears filled my eyes and clung to my lower lashes, and I wiped them with the edge of my blanket.

Max came and sat close, his hand reaching out to rest on my forearm. "Don't give up hope yet, okay?"

I smiled through the tears. "Don't worry. I haven't given up. Where did you go? Getting some awful hospital lunch?"

He chuckled. "Not quite. I was on the phone with Ethan."

My heart warmed over. "Does he forgive me?"

Max didn't answer, and icy doubt trickled through my veins.

"I think you two should talk about that when you're able." He patted my arm, and I changed the subject.

"Roy and Gypsy are coming to visit. They're bringing you some real food." I squeezed his hand, and he let out a laugh.

"Great, I was worried about the cafeteria food again." Max rubbed his gut. The almost unnoticeable wince caught my attention.

"I'm sorry you're hurting."

He shook his head. "Don't you worry about me, I'm fine. A bit sore is all."

I didn't know what else to say. The nice thing about Max was I didn't have to talk. We could sit in silence and be fine.

"Max, tell me how Ethan is." I needed to know.

He shook his head. "You'll have to ask him."

Somehow, I'd known Max would say that, and something occurred to me at that moment; I'd rather have Ethan sitting in the room with me, his attention on his work, than not here at all. For all the times I teased him about his workaholic ways, he'd always been there, regardless. And it meant a lot that he ignored work to spend time with me. He focused on me while we were together, and the significance didn't escape me. I'd give anything to see him walk in, nose to tablet, pausing only to flash me that heart-melting smile.

The door slid open, and my doctor stormed in like a ball of fire, crackling energy everywhere. "Your numbers are good, and everything is ready. We need to get you prepped for surgery."

Prepped for surgery?

"You found a donor?" I couldn't believe the news. I expected to go months before finding a match.

The doc smiled and nodded as the nurses undid the brakes

on my bed and wheeled me toward the door. Max stayed at my side as we rolled out, and I stared up at him. "Did you know about this?" His comment about not giving up made more sense.

He nodded, and the hospital passed in a blur. Up in the elevator, I lost track of where we'd gone as they wheeled me into a room. My whole being called out for Ethan as the team prepped me. I saw Max being led away, and the loneliness of not having my family near hollowed me out. I kept those I loved in my mind as the surgical team prepped.

The things that truly mattered were the people I loved, the people who came through for me, like Roy and Gypsy, promising to be family even though Roy wasn't my biological father, and Gypsy was his girlfriend with no relation to me either. Max and his unconditional love and support—a long time coming, but through no fault of his own—he mattered. Ethan's kindness, taking care of me when I needed him the most. Those were the people that stayed in my heart.

Life was all about relationships, love, and family, the ones we kept close.

The nurse spoke above me. "You're going to feel very sleepy. Please count backward from ten."

"Ten..."

"Nine..."

"Eigh ... Ethan."

I FELT as though I was swimming through cotton-soaked water. I saw the hazy surface, but I didn't feel liquid on my skin. Muted, distorted voices surrounded me, along with a somber sense of dread. Maybe I was drowning, not swimming.

The urge to fight kicked in, and I struggled toward the light and sound. Blinking at the brightness, I heard noises around me slip into sharp focus as the room finally made sense.

I was in a hospital room, and I'd undergone surgery.

"She's awake." Gypsy's excited voice halted the buzz of conversation, and I glanced over at her. She, Roy, and Max moved toward me.

"How are you?" Gypsy gathered up my hands, and I noticed the worry mingling with hope in her eyes.

Someone had donated a kidney and everyone rallied behind me and promised to support me in any way possible.

"I'm good. I mean, I can't feel anything, but that's good, right?" My body seemed numb like I was nothing more than a floating head.

Max chuckled. "That's probably the drugs. We'll call the doctor in to check you out. While we wait, maybe you should thank your donor." He nodded to the other side of me, and I rolled my head and caught sight of Ethan stretched out on the bed next to mine. His tired smile and dark smudges under his eyes surprised me.

"Hi," I whispered, not sure what else to say.

"Hi." His voice stirred something deep within me as all the pieces fell into place.

"You donated your kidney for me?" It couldn't be possible, but as I studied his expression and the way his powerful body looked on the hospital bed, the same worn blankets that didn't help me, and barely covered him, showed me the truth. Ethan had saved my life.

He nodded.

What could I say? "Thank you." Focusing all my strength, I inched my fingers toward him, letting my arm slide off the bed as I reached out. He did the same, seeming to move easier than I, and his pinkie finger hooked around mine.

"You're welcome," he whispered as Roy, Gypsy, and Max all talked amongst themselves, waving down a nurse and standing at the door to my room.

I spent so much time worrying that he might not forgive me, yet there he was, in the bed next to me, recovering after having given me one of his kidneys and a new chance at life.

"Did Max tell you about his wife?" Did he know the risk he'd taken for me?

He nodded, and his serious expression left no doubt that he knew his kindness could have cost him his life.

CHAPTER TWENTY-FOUR

ETHAN

HER DELICATE FEATURES and thin frame under the sheet terrified me. I swear she dropped weight in the few days since I'd seen her last. Still, she looked beautiful.

"I'm sorry I didn't tell you." Her soft voice held my attention as I saw Max glance over his shoulder at us, wink, then shuffle the other two out of the room. Of course, he wanted us to have time to talk—no doubt he hoped we'd patch things up and get back together.

I wouldn't let him know, but that was a possibility I wouldn't throw away.

"I understand." I meant my words.

Her eyes widened. "You understand?"

The hope in her voice broke my heart. I could tell she wanted me to understand her and that she'd done what she had for important reasons. That distinction became a focal point for me. I didn't have to think her motivations were good enough—they were enough for her; therefore, they were simply enough.

"I'm sorry for being such a jerk, and I'm sorry for not being there when you needed me. I'm sorry for being cruel and saying you manufactured things between us. That was uncalled for, and I regret those words." I meant that with every fiber of my being. As I studied her, I watched her shoulders lift as if a weight had come off them.

"Ethan, you are here when I needed you." Her delicate voice left my heart beating harder as her smile grew and her gaze caressed mine. "It means more to me than I can ever explain."

Her sweet words were the world to me, but there were things I needed to get out of my head. "I understand why you came to Cross Creek and why you kept it to yourself, but I hope you can trust me now." I couldn't fault her if she didn't trust me anymore, not after how I ended things and ditched her when she needed me most.

"Ethan," she said, her frail voice making me nervous as her wide eyes studied my face, "Can we start over?"

I understood what she wanted, but starting over wasn't an option. "I don't think so."

Her expression fell, and I knew I needed to explain myself.

"I don't want to start over. I have feelings for you, Angie. Strong feelings that can't go back to the beginning. I don't want to dance around our attraction to each other. I want to go back to the night I made love to you."

She visibly relaxed, and her smile reappeared like the sun from behind dark clouds. "It sure felt like love."

"Let's start from there, but with honesty as our guide."

"Okay, your turn to be honest." She cocked her head. "Did Max talk you into donating your kidney to me?"

That sounded like Max. He spent this entire time trying to

guide me to be a better person, to make the right choices, and to be someone I could be proud of, but he never asked for my kidney. "Actually, no, but he said something that hit me kind of hard." I could still hear his voice as he said the words. "He said, 'I'd give her my kidney if I could. I don't want to lose her when I just found her.'"

Tears instantly sparkled in her eyes.

"It doesn't matter that he didn't raise you or that he missed out on big milestones in your life. Max is all in, Angie. He already loves you like a daughter." She deserved that fatherly love she'd been denied all her life.

"Thank you, Ethan." Her pinkie released mine, then brushed my hand a few times. "Hey, I'm getting feeling back."

"What happens now?" I asked her.

She lifted a shoulder. "Whatever you want to happen, I guess."

I realized I hadn't been clear enough and made a mental note to work on my communication skills and clarity. If we were going to make us work, I needed to express myself better.

"I mean with the kidney, does this give you more time, or...?" I trailed off, scared of the possibility that down the road, she'd need another one.

She stared at me, eyes round, mouth rounder. "You honestly don't know?"

I shook my head. I didn't know.

"A healthy kidney transplant doesn't grow cysts. Barring some terrible accident, this kidney gives me another shot at a normal life." The excitement in her voice dimmed. "Of course, the meds I have to take to stop my body from rejecting the transplant are not a picnic, but it's better than the alternative." She lowered her voice. "I thought I'd spend the rest of my life in one of these beds."

I ached for her. The thought of trading places with her and being the one afraid to live out the rest of my days at such a young age on this hospital bed was terrifying. How fortunate I'd been to never worry about my health.

Something protective in me reared up. I wanted to take care of her. Could I be the one to pick her up when she fell? To bathe her when she couldn't shower alone? I didn't mind holding back her hair when she threw up.

And it hit me; that's what *in sickness and in health* truly meant. She was worth the sick days, the difficult days, the days we were both at our worst.

I wouldn't rush into things. We'd take everything slowly. For now, at least.

Everyone stepped back into the room, and the doctor followed. I watched over him as he checked on Angie. His body language seemed positive, more than his cautiously optimistic words, and I knew his conservative tone had more to do with not overselling her health.

While they checked me out, I couldn't take my eyes off her as her family gathered in close, talking, laughing, and giving her careful hugs. Roy had stepped up and agreed to be her dad, though he wasn't related by blood or anything else for that matter. Gypsy … she'd become family too. And Max? I meant it when I said he was all in. He'd be her dad until the end of time.

"Oh, and Isla's project," Gypsy said. "She got an A-plus."

"That's amazing." Angie's voice shone through the room.

The doctor smiled at me, his expression calm. "Everything

looks good. You focus on healing, and you'll be out of here in no time."

I thanked him quietly, and he left while I watched Angie smile, surrounded by all the love she'd found.

"What are you thinking about?" Max's attention shifted to me as Angie and Gypsy continued talking.

"That I should've listened to you from the beginning." I wasn't willing to let her go. Not without a fight and a solid stab at a relationship.

Max chuckled. "I worried I'd never hear you say that."

"Don't get too used to it and don't you dare tell anyone." I didn't care if he shouted from the mountain tops that I finally came to my senses. Max wasn't that kind of guy, and I wasn't ashamed to admit I'd grown as a human being.

"Your dad would be proud of you, son. And he'd love Angie, I'm sure." Max's fatherly tone stabbed through me like an arrow.

"You're just saying that because you're her father." I loved the pride in his face while he talked about her as we both watched her and Gypsy talk in animated tones.

Angie glanced at me out of the corner of her eyes while Gypsy pulled her phone out of her pocket, saying she had pictures. That look gave me a glimpse into a future with her by my side, a future I'd love to have.

"Well, you might be right." Max chuckled.

When Angie glanced at me, I knew she saw a future with me too.

"Finally. Here I thought you were always right." I nudged Max with a numb elbow, and he batted my arm away.

"Maybe we're both right. How about that?" He lifted both dark brows, and I realized I liked the sound of that.

EPILOGUE
ANGIE - A FEW MONTHS LATER...

I GLANCED AROUND THE TABLE, stunned at the turn my life had taken. Ethan's mom, Irene, sat at the head of the table, looking as beautiful as ever. Around me sat Noah and Kandra.

Kandra's adorable pregnant belly had me wanting to rub it, but I'd never touch her without her permission.

Kandra and Miranda sat side by side, head-to-head, talking in low voices. Next to Sheriff Miranda, Bayden and Quinn kicked one another under the table like adolescent boys. Quinn held little Kip, who stared at his uncle while he explained the politics of beating up your brother when he deserved it, which prompted Kandra to lift her head and chastise him. "Quinn."

Quinn lifted his head, giving her an innocent stare as she and Miranda focused on him like lionesses ready to smack down a male cub that had gotten too big for his britches.

"Don't teach him that," Miranda added.

Quinn smiled, and Gypsy reached over and took Kip from him while he focused on his brothers' wives.

Gypsy talked to Kip, and he stared at her, mesmerized, while Roy made faces at the little one.

Beside them, Max glanced at me, his gaze sparkling as he nodded to the other side of me. I glanced over and met Ethan's eyes. There was no tablet in his hand and no phone hidden under the table where his mother couldn't see. He stared at me as if I was the only thing in the world he wanted to see.

"Is there something on my face?" I whispered.

He shook his head, his smile growing. "I haven't seen my mother this happy since ... goodness knows when."

"How long do we have?" I glanced at my phone, seeing the group texts from the rest of my family. In a few minutes, something was going down, and Quinn and Irene had no idea what was happening next. That made me oddly happy. This moment reminded me of what I thought Christmas morning should feel like.

"I don't know." Ethan's shrug told me he hadn't been watching the time because he was too busy watching me.

"When are you going to find someone, Quinn?" Irene's sweet voice and smile didn't fool me for a second. She wanted to make sure her last son found someone sooner rather than later.

"Did anyone ever tell Quinn Max's story?" Bayden seemed to pity his twin and changed the subject as the smell of food floated through the air. We sat down with our drinks and some finger foods, waiting on the turkey they cooked up.

Quinn paused. "Max's story?"

Max also studied Bayden before meeting Quinn's gaze. "You mean about my late wife?"

Bayden nodded, his attention bouncing from one to the other as Miranda patted his hand.

Max wiped his hands on his napkin with a thoughtful look while speaking up for a confused Quinn. "He already knew."

The other brothers glanced at one another. "What? But he can't keep a secret," Noah said as Kandra rested her head on his shoulder in a sweet gesture. Beside me, Ethan put a hand on my knee, and I smiled at him.

Max lifted his shoulders. "He knew long before any of you."

Beside me, Ethan let out a stunned snort. Noah's mouth dropped open, and Bayden threw his napkin on the table in front of him, earning him a glare from his mother and a light smack from Miranda. "We didn't tell him because we thought he'd blow the secret." Bayden's mock anger earned a chuckle from the women, and Quinn's offended stare spoke volumes.

"I knew Quinn was trustworthy, and he proved he could keep a secret—maybe better than you, Bayden." Max lifted his brows and took a sip of his drink as people around the table grinned and glanced at one another, loving his poke at the twin.

I loved this entire exchange—the sight of Kip in Gypsy's arms as Roy stuck his tongue out at the little one. The toddler's laughter and the buzz of conversation left me feeling more at home than I ever had.

Ethan's hand left my knee, and his arm slipped around my shoulder. He pulled me close, and I leaned into him. Irene had invited my family into her home. She'd been sweet, and everyone treated me, Max, Roy, and Gypsy, like actual flesh-and-blood kin. Heck, they treated me more like family than my mom had.

"You okay?" Ethan's whispered voice earned him a smile, and I nodded.

It was a lie. I was more than okay. I'd never been happier.

Ethan and I were making strides as a couple, and we were solid, building on concrete instead of sand, as he'd say.

Max treated me like the daughter he never had. Roy did too, and Gypsy was the mom I could call every day and talk to about everything and nothing. And finally, everyone stopped wearing baseball caps around me, proving they'd forgiven me for stealing their DNA.

Everything was fabulous. "I'm perfect. What about you?"

He pulled me into his arms. "I love you, Angie. I should've said it weeks ago, but I've been keeping secrets."

My pulse kicked up.

"That's a secret I don't mind, but I'm glad you told me. I love you too," I whispered.

"I've got another one."

What was he hiding from me?

"Ethan Lockhart. What aren't you telling me?"

Conversation stopped, and all eyes were on us.

Ethan stood and cleared his throat.

"It's about time," Max said. My father seemed to know everything.

Ethan glanced at his family and grinned before he pulled a box from his pocket and presented me with a simple solitaire mounted in yellow gold. He took a knee, and after all the oohs and ahs from his family, he said, "Be mine?"

I smiled at him. "I always have been. Don't forget ... I chose you first."

He slipped the ring on my finger, and we all celebrated with hugs and kisses before the doorbell rang.

Poor Quinn was in for it. He was the last brother standing, but would he stand for long with his meddling family?

Noah opened the door to Lauren. She peeked inside with eyes wide at the massive gathering.

"Hello," she breathed, glancing at us, then back at Noah. "I'm here about the job? My name is Lauren."

"Of course, this way." He led her into the dining room. And I felt bad for the poor woman. She was being considered for the accounting job the guys needed filled after the last guy retired. Everyone but Quinn had been in on hiring her, and the entire family's matchmaking senses were on high alert. Now that I'd seen her, I could see why his family thought she'd be perfect. She was exactly his type.

Her thick blonde ponytail hung down her back, and her button-down lilac shirt and black slacks gave her a professional air, as did the dark leather bag hanging from her shoulder.

She walked inside, introducing herself to everyone with a sense of bravery I didn't possess as I leaned against Ethan and stared at my ring.

"It's nice to meet all of you," she said, clasping her hands in front of her and rising on the balls of her feet more than her heels already had her doing.

I peeked at Quinn out of the corner of my eye. Usually, he handled interviews, which was why the guys had taken this over. Quinn would've hired an old, bald man who posed no risk to his heart.

The brothers were looking to set the fair-haired twin up. He stared at her, stunned, then his eyes narrowed as he took in each one of his siblings. Yep, he knew what they were up to.

"Please join us." Noah offered Lauren a seat, and she took it.

"Credentials? Years of experience? Letters of recommendation?" Quinn's quick-fire questions earned him a glare from his mother.

"Quinn, don't be rude." Irene's smile softened as she glanced at the woman. "I don't know what's gotten into him. This is a family business, started by my late husband, Kip."

"I'm truly sorry for your loss." Lauren's heartfelt smile locked on Irene seemed to make an impression on the matriarch. "However … I have everything you asked for." She reached into her bag, but Irene stopped her.

"Please, not at the table. We'd like to make sure you can handle us before putting you through the gauntlet of a formal interview. Tonight, you're simply our guest. Allow me to introduce everyone." Irene began introductions as Ethan squeezed my knee.

On my other side, Max patted my shoulder, and I smiled at him as Gypsy passed Kip around the table. The little one stopped on my lap, and I stared into his dark-blue eyes. Ethan knew having children together wasn't in the cards. We talked about it many times, but he still wanted me, regardless. We might not be parents, but we'd be the best aunt and uncle this beautiful boy could have. "How are you, little one?" I asked softly not to interrupt the introductions.

Kip flashed an enormous smile, showing off his dimples and melting my heart. This beautiful little boy didn't stand a chance. Between all of us, he'd be spoiled and never want for anything. I could be jealous that he'd have everything I ever wanted, but I was spoiled too. The Lockhart family made up for everything my life had lacked.

Kip snuggled into my arms, Ethan held my knee, and Irene introduced me as her daughter. I smiled, knowing I ended up exactly where I should be. Cross Creek *had* held the answers to my missing father's whereabouts. In the end, not only had I gained a father but also the family I always longed to have.

Next Up is Reckless Hart

AFTERWORD

Dear Reader,

    If you are interested in finding out more about polycystic kidney disease, please visit https://pkdcure.org/. While I tried to portray an authentic experience by talking with patients and medical staff in my research, I am not an expert or a physician, and this is a work of fiction written to entertain. I hope you loved Ethan's and Angie's story and will venture to book four to see how Quinn fares in the game of love.

    Always choose love,
    Kelly

SNEEK PEEK AT RECKLESS HART
LAUREN

Dinner with the Lockharts went well, but I'm pretty sure Quinn doesn't like me.

Especially after I pointed out an unpaid debt I'd uncovered during my 'trial' that I'd offered Noah to prove I was serious about the job—Quinn swore that debt had been paid, but he was wrong.

While pulling my keys from my purse, I strolled up the front walk to the little cottage I'd rented, thinking this was the strangest Sunday I'd experienced in a long time. I threw a cautious glance over my shoulder as the sensation of being watched prickled up my neck. Smoothing a hand over the spot, I faced the charcoal-colored door and hurried up the three concrete steps to the little wooden porch, still reminiscing about the frustrating, good-looking, blond Lockhart brother.

All I could do was follow the numbers, but I swear Quinn seemed ready to fight tooth and nail to prove I didn't know what I was talking about and that I shouldn't get the job. His brothers all seemed to think I'd be an asset to the team, which left me certain that Quinn thought if I didn't get the job, they could talk their old accountant into staying. Why else would he be dead set against them hiring me? He didn't strike me as sexist, and nothing he said led me to believe he had something personal against me. He'd merely stated that Ol' Brock was a good guy. He was who his dearly departed father had hired and trusted, and he knew how to run things. Clearly, Quinn didn't like change. Well, changes were coming if I had anything to say about it. But that would never happen if they asked me for my letter of recommendation, which luckily they didn't do—yet.

Sliding my key into the lock on the front door, I stumbled a bit as I was still getting used to the place. A brand-new home in a new town where my daughter Fawn and I would start our lives together. Would everything finally settle down and let me breathe?

I'd been to Cross Creek before because my grandparents, Norman and Ethel, lived here. Even though I'd only ever visited, I loved this little town.

I exhaled as the lock clicked slightly and the deadbolt retracted. Turning the handle and pressing the door open, I stepped into the living room. No light from the TV, no sound from the kitchen, no noise at all left me nervously touring my own home.

Opening a bedroom door, I saw Missy put a finger to her lips as she cradled my four-year-old daughter, Fawn. With a smile, I motioned for Missy to come on out. She'd been my best friend for as long as I could remember, and when she found out I was moving to Cross Creek, she packed up her life and moved to Silver Springs to stay close to Fawn and me.

I watched her carefully untangle from Fawn's sweaty, sleeping embrace and stand slowly, testing the floor as if not trusting the hardwood not to squeak. Like a villain from a cartoon, she tiptoed in my direction, hands in front, dangling like T-Rex arms, her knees coming to her chest with each step.

Her messy black curls and bright blue eyes reminded me of the color of my mother's, and I smiled at her playful expression. We crept out of my daughter's room as if we were teenagers sneaking out of the house for a party featuring alcohol and boys.

"How did it go?" Missy slung an arm around my shoulders and squeezed me as we headed into the kitchen. She inhaled as she took in the budget furniture I'd filled the place with. As she ran a fingertip along the ugly, cheap table, I tried not to imagine the beautiful things I had in my previous home.

I didn't think about it before. Not unless I had to.

I let out a sigh while grabbing the wine out of the house-warming basket my mother had sent. Missy pulled the bottle opener out of the drawer, and I smiled at her, wondering how the heck she knew where I kept it.

She must have read my expression because she glanced at the drawer, then scanned the tiny kitchen. "I mean, it's the most logical place." She reached for the fridge. "It's near the fridge and close to the glasses," she demonstrated, "and this place would turn me into an alcoholic quickly."

I laughed, scanning the dingy kitchen. The house could use some updating and a heavy-handed deep clean, but I didn't hate it. "I know it's not pretty, but it's growing on me." I took in an exaggerated breath. "Smells like home. Freedom. A fresh new start."

She snatched the wine bottle from me and opened it, her eyebrows trying to march up to her forehead and off her face. "That smell is black mold."

I laughed again as a clickity-clacking noise turned me toward the door. "Lucky!" My daughter's tiny one-eyed, snaggle-toothed, wire-haired terrier came trotting up to me, his tongue hanging out of his mouth to the right, so long I worried—as I always did—that he might trip over the darn thing.

I crouched down to pet him, and he did a little dance with his front feet before lifting one leg and curling the pad of his paw back. She'd picked this winner out at the pound after hearing that the ugly dogs tended not to find loving homes, and she'd shown him every bit of love a dog could have—the two were partners in crime and damned near inseparable.

Missy offered some wine, and I stood up, took it from her, and made my way to the table. Sitting in one of the chairs, I sipped the sweet red. "I think I'll be happy here." I stared at the wineglass, then began to rotate it by the stem. The glass warped the room beyond as Lucky came trotting over and flopped under my chair. Within seconds, the small dog was snoring so loud you'd think a bear found its way into my kitchen.

"I hope you will. You deserve to be happy." She smiled at me past the tiny bit of wine she'd poured for herself.

"You could take an Uber home and leave your car. No worries." She was the type of responsible that didn't like to drive after a single sip of wine, a trait I respected, and it wouldn't be the first time she took an Uber home from my place.

She shook her head. "I promised my mom I'd take her to her class tomorrow. She's not ready to trust any driving services."

I giggled. Missy's mom didn't trust anyone, let alone a stranger that would take her places for money. And every time, she'd go off on a tangent about these new services that have people willingly getting into rapist's and murderer's cars, but she's quick to quiet down when reminded taxis still exist. Still, her mother is fun and sweet, even if she's opinionated.

"Are you going to be okay?" Her stare weighed me down, and I knew she'd see right through a lie. So, I told her the truth.

"I think so." I didn't have a more concrete answer than that—not yet. I had Fawn and a roof over my head as well as a job prospect and a fresh start. Barring any disasters, I thought I would be fine. Lucky let out an ungodly snort that shook him awake. He glared at Missy for a moment as if she'd woken him up, then promptly went back to sleep.

"And this job, do you think it's a sure thing?"

I didn't know the answer to that. Quinn seemed very adamant about not hiring me. I felt deflated. The second I turned in my letter of recommendation, he'd find out the truth.

"You don't seem very confident." Missy's troubled tone had me flashing a false smile. I didn't want her to worry about me.

"Oh, I've got the job." Over Quinn's dead body, I'd bet. No doubt he'd spend the entire night trying to explain why I wasn't a good fit for the company and that hiring me would ruin everything the guys had worked so hard and long for. I downed the rest of my wine and set the empty glass on the table.

"Well, okay then. Give me hugs. I have to get home." She finished her wine before flinging her arms wide toward me. I stood up to hug her, noticing that she squeezed me extra tight for a second before letting go. Her gaze met mine. "You've got this. You're amazing at what you do, and those guys would be fools not to hire you. And if they're all hot..." She winked.

"Hot and married." Or dating, at least, except for Quinn. Of course, the one guy that seemed to hate my guts on sight would be the most sinfully attractive *and* the only available guy. "Besides, I'm not looking for love. I swore off men, remember?"

Miss knew me well enough to know that if I said something, I meant it. And I meant it when I said I was abstaining from guys for the foreseeable future. I didn't want to get hurt again, and the only way I could ensure that was strictly staying away.

"Ugh. You're too young and hot to be single." She headed for the door, and I followed on her heels.

"Then why don't you date me?" I teased as she opened the front door and turned to me, a grin on her face.

"I might! Especially if you're going to be a stubborn ass about it!" She planted a hand on her hip, then quickly pulled me in for another hug. "It's flipping cold out here! I'm gonna run out and turn the heater on." A moment later, she trotted down the walk toward her car, her breath silver in the air as darkness drowned out the last bit of light, coloring the horizon a brilliant pink.

Her little car roared to life, and I could hear her cussing as she ran the heat, no doubt telling the car to hurry the frick up and get warm.

With a chuckle, I closed the door and noticed Lucky staring at me. "Need to go out?" I asked, waiting for him to give me an answer.

He tilted his head back and forth for a few minutes, as if deciding, then walked toward Fawn's room, no doubt to climb into her warm bed and hide under the covers with his best friend. I smiled at the overload of cuteness that thought brought me and padded back into the kitchen. Pouring myself another glass of wine, I tried to stifle the unease settling into my being.

The letter of recommendation in my bag seemed to be mocking me. Like some pendulum heartbeat under the floorboards, it taunted me from the other room, and I gulped down my wine in an unladylike swallow.

What would happen when I had to give them that letter from my previous job? Would Quinn see right through my ruse? Would he know I forged the letter? Because I hadn't quit my last job for a Fortune 500 company on good terms, as I'd claimed in the letter.

No, I'd been fired through no fault of my own. Well, not really my fault, anyway. I hadn't personally done anything fire-able, so I did what I thought I had to do to secure another job; I wrote the letter of recommendation myself.

What else could I do? Pouring another glass, I stared at a spot on the shabby laminate floors. I brought both arms close to my chest as if that would simulate the hug I desperately needed as I thought about how quickly my seemingly perfect life had fallen apart.

My wine sloshed dangerously near the rim as someone knocked at the door—the hard knock of a cop ready to bust in and make arrests as dread filled my belly.

GET A FREE BOOK.

Go to www.authorkellycollins.com

ALSO BY BY KELLY COLLINS

An Aspen Cove Romance Series

One Hundred Reasons

One Hundred Heartbeats

One Hundred Wishes

One Hundred Promises

One Hundred Excuses

Cross Creek Novels

Broken Hart

Fearless Hart

Guarded Hart

Reckless Hart

ABOUT THE AUTHOR

International bestselling author of more than thirty novels, Kelly Collins writes with the intention of keeping love alive. Always a romantic, she blends real-life events with her vivid imagination to create characters and stories that lovers of contemporary romance, new adult, and romantic suspense will return to again and again.

For More Information
www.authorkellycollins.com
kelly@authorkellycollins.com